The Royals on Keeper Hill

Written by

Poppy G. Pleazing

(pseudonym)

AuthorHouse™ UK
1663 Liberty Drive
Bloomington, IN 47403 USA
www.authorhouse.co.uk
UK TFN: 0800 0148641 (Toll Free inside the UK)
UK Local: 02036 956322 (+44 20 3695 6322 from outside the UK)

Because of the dynamic nature of the Internet, any web addresses or links contained in this book may have changed
since publication and may no longer be valid. The views expressed in this work are solely those of the author and do not
necessarily reflect the views of the publisher, and the publisher hereby disclaims any responsibility for them.

Any people depicted in stock imagery provided by Getty Images are models,
and such images are being used for illustrative purposes only.
Certain stock imagery © Getty Images.

This book is printed on acid-free paper.

ISBN: 978-1-6655-8336-7 (sc)
ISBN: 978-1-6655-8337-4 (e)

Print information available on the last page.

Published by AuthorHouse 01/22/2021

authorHOUSE®

Wonderful Adventures

from

The Royals

on

Keeper Hill

in the

County of Tipperary

in the

Land of Truth and Happiness

Poppy G. Pleazing

Introduction to the Family and characters.

This selection of short stories, will bring you, your children and your grandchildren, into a wonderful, magical land. These spectacular adventures, can be read to and by anyone, from the age of understanding, to approximately 100 years. I'm not kidding. They bring out the wonderful world of children in all, no matter how old we think we are. They are also suited for children, between the ages of six and ten years for self reading.

Each story, is centred around the royal family and their friends, who live in a wonderful land. This Queendom, as it is called, because it is ruled by Queen Rainbow, is situated in the magical county of Tipperary, in the Land of Truth and Happiness. Rainbow Village, is also called after the Queen and it is the shopping centre, of the queendom. The village, is made up of one main street and a couple of avenues, lined with brightly, painted shops and houses. This is where, day to day business takes place. Each story, is set on a definite day, in a definite month and are most definitely true, in the minds of those, who need a little mystic, mystery and magic, in their lives.

Rainbow Palace, is the home of Queen Rainbow and King Jack, who are the royal children's grandparents. It is also the home of Nani, who helps with the welfare and rearing, of the royal children. The palace, high on Keeper Hill, overlooks the great Queendom of Keeper Valley, surrounded by many hills, streams and farmlands. Keeper Queendom, consists of four royal estates. Rainbow is the largest. The other three are called Richmond, Sleeper Cottage and Ashford. The royal family consists of Queen Rainbow, King Jack and Nani. There are three mommies, three daddies and eight royal grandchildren, all first cousins. There are two dogs, named Flip and Flop. There are many chickens, birds, rabbits, goldfish and cats, at least one bear and one octopus.

Rainbow Palace, is painted, gold and blue. It has two rainbow-coloured towers, reaching to the sky. There are diamonds on the walls and pearls around each window. There are crystal snowdrops, drooping from the ceilings and sparkles and sprinkles on the floors. It has two playrooms. The first one has shelves of wonderful toys, books, building blocks and puzzles. The other playroom is filled with every kind of soft, fluffy cuddly, toy imaginable. Some of these can sing. Others can dance and move about and do fun things. The royal gardens, which are situated at the back of the Rainbow Palace, are full of magnificent colourful pastures, of poppies, wheat and sweet pea. There is a secret meadow and a magical forest, where Brown Bear and many other animals live. Along the edge of the forest, there is a dark narrow passage, where the royal children, are forbidden to venture. But they go there sometimes, because this passage leads down to the lake and river, into which Oxy Octopus, Silky Seal, Dafty Dolphin and many other sea-creatures, swim in from the sea, from time to time, to rest on the rocks.

The scents and sounds from the gardens, from all the flowers, birds, bees, butterflies and rabbits, are wonderful. The royal playground near the palace, has swings, roundabouts and a great climbing frame, upon which Gwen, Isaac and Noah love to climb. Those three children, are like little monkeys when they are in the garden. Gwen climbs, more than any other child I have ever met and if she is not climbing, she is doing cartwheels on the lawn, with her cousin Lola. On the hill, nearest to the palace, among the apple trees, there is a secret garden. It cannot be seen from anywhere on the estate, not even from the sky. Only the adult members of the royal family, know the secret entrance and the passcode.

Richmond Residence, is a beautiful villa, just one kilometre beyond Rainbow village. This Villa is painted cream and red. It smells like vanilla and strawberries. It has a long drive-way leading to the main entrance, that is lined with yellow daffodils. It is the home of **prince Alex, prince Evan and princess Zoe**. Their parents are Duke Michael and Duchess Caroline. Their step cousins, who sometimes come to visit are Mr. and Mrs. T. and little prince Ned.

Ashford Manor, is a wonderful country dwelling, in the valley between Rainbow Village and Keeper Hill. It is painted purple and white and surrounded by poppy fields. This is where **princess Lola and prince Noah** live with their parents, Lord Jesse, and Lady Sara.

Sleeper-Cottage Castle, is a grand castle, built among wild, lavender bushes, in the hills above Rainbow Village. There are two cherry-blossom trees in the front garden. It is built with pink and peach, spongy stones and smells like marshmallows. It is the home of **princess Penelope, princess Gwen and prince Isaac**. They live with their parents, Countess Kasey and Earl Matthew. Sleeper-Cottage Castle, is the closest domicile to Queen Rainbow and King Jack's Royal Palace

Keeper Queendom, is the most wonderful place to live. It is filled with honest, kind, friendly people and animals. Everyone knows everyone else. Everyone accepts everyone else, no matter how odd or different from each other they might seem. Queen Rainbow, is kind and tolerant. She smiles and chats to the village dwellers and the shop owners, when she goes shopping, or when she visits the hairdresser and the florist. Her husband, King Jack, is a fusspot, about flowers. He spends his days planting new flowers and shrubs. He loves their scent and colours. He checks frequently, that the flowers are in perfect rows, in the royal gardens. Keeper Queendom, is made up of valleys, forests and farmland, surrounded by great hills and streams. It is situated, not too far from the ocean. In fact, if you go to the top of the Royal Palace, the very tip top, to the royal-rainbow-lookout tower, you can see far and wide. You can even see the green-blue ocean, in the distance. You can see sailing boats and dolphins. You can also see the people of Rainbow Village, going about their daily business. They are, the butcher Mr. Lamb, the baker Mr. Crusty and little Miss Mix, who owns the supermarket. There is also Miss Weed, the friendly widow, who runs the village florist. On a clear blue day, you can see the rows of trees, along Great Uncle Gerry's drive, leading up to his grand home and gardens. He lives sixteen kilometres away, on the far side of Rainbow Village.

Outside the main entrance of Rainbow Palace, there is the downhill, winding road, with many tree-tunnels and hidden pathways, leading to the main road, down to the valley and into the village, full of rainbow shops and wonderful restaurants.

Once more, I would like to stress, that these stories, are very real events, in the minds, in which they flourish, especially in the mind of Nani.

Sometimes, the names of the children are real and other times the children choose fictional names. All the stories are definitely, really-true, great adventures, that took place in the Queendom of Keeper Hill, in the county of Tipperary, in the Land of Truth and Happiness.

Poppy G. Pleazing.

Contents

Mister Sun can't Sleep

Mister Sun, bright and orange, sat on top of the highest mountain and his rays poured down on Keeper Queendom, in the County of Tipperary in The Land of Truth and Happiness.

I think it was a Wednesday in September?

He could not sleep. He just wasn't tired enough to set. He thought about staying up all night and watching the stars twinkle.

Down on Keeper hill and in the surrounding areas, the children were getting ready for bed. Their cousins in Ashford and Richmond, were also cuddling in for the night. Princess Gwen, wore a pretty pink nightie. Her older sister, princess Penelope, and her younger brother, prince Isaac, were in their cosy pyjamas. They had each just finished a tumbler of warm milk and oat cookies.

They brushed their teeth, before choosing one bedtime story each. Gwen chose *Nani's Red Car*, Penelope chose *Zoe and the Rabbit Hole* and Isaac wanted to hear *Oxy and Jammy*, because this was his favourite. The three children sat on their beds, while mommy read clearly, with great exitement in her voice. They loved when it was mommy's turn to read. She was the best story-teller. Her voice helped them make pictures in their heads of all the wonderful things happening in the story. Sometimes mommy didn't even need a story book. She just created the most wonderful adventures from her imagination. Daddy kissed the children goodnight. He tucked all three in, under their duvets, with their favourite bed buddies, who were Pink Mousey, Brown Bunny and Blue Bunny.

It was unusually bright outside. There was a beam of light shining between the gap in the curtain and the wall. The children were restless. It should be getting dark, they thought, as it was way past time for Mister Sun to set.

The animals, who live in the Land of Truth and Happiness, in fact the animals all over the world, were confused. You see they don't have clocks to tell the time and they don't wear watches and I have never seen a big, brown bear with a mobile phone. The animals only know it is bedtime, when the sun sets, when the stars twinkle in the sky and when the big man in the moon shines. No one knew what was going on, this bright evening, except Mr. Sun, who just sat on the mountain top, gazing down at the world. He was very quiet. He didn't even sink a little. He just wouldn't go down.

He smiled down on the world, shining his bright rays. He was pleased, at how beautiful everything looked, in the bright light. He began to wonder what everything would look like, if there was no light. He had never seen dark. He didn't know what dark was and he was curious about that now.

Mister Man-in-the-Moon was not happy, nor were the thousand stars, waiting to twinkle in the sky. They could not be seen while the Mister Sun was still shining his bright, dazzling light.

"Mister Sun," shouted Man-in-the-Moon very loud. "You have to go to sleep now and let me shine in the night sky and, and, and, let the stars twinkle," he said with a stutter. "All the boys and girls and animals are, are, are tired and they need to s s sleep. They cannot sleep with you still s s shining. You really need to set now please."

"Yes," squealed a thousand stars. "We want to dance around the sky. The children can't see where we are. They won't be able to sing their favourite song" and with that the stars started to sing.

"*Twinkle, twinkle little star, how I wonder what you are*

Up above the world so high, like a diamond in the sky."

"Oh shush," said Mister Sun very loud, "I'm not tired, so I won't be going to bed tonight. Now don't bother me"

"Oh, my goodness," said Mister Fluffy, the white cloud, as he shyly passed by. "Oh, my goodness indeed, Mister Sun," repeated Mister Fluffy. "All you have to do now is sink and in the morning, you have to rise. That is all you have to do every day. Don't go making things complicated, for everyone. Sink now, please and let everyone go to sleep. It is your duty. That's all you have to do every night, just go down and sleep."

The children on Keeper Hill were yawning; yawn, yawn, yawn, but sleep did not find them. Their bedroom was much too bright, even with the curtains drawn.

"I wonder what is going on outside," said Penelope to her little brother and sister. "I cannot see the stars on our ceiling window twinkle, because it is still too bright."

Up in the sky there was still some confusion. "I'm not tired," repeated Mister Sun. "I want to stay and see the stars."

"Well, I never," said Mister Fluffy. "You can never see the stars. Don't you know, that if you shine, the stars can't twinkle. They are invisible in your light, Mister Sun. It's just the way night and day is, just the way the world is and that's a fact and can't be any other way." He thought for a minute." Maybe I could stand in front of you and take away some of that brightness and let the stars, shine a little. That might work."

Mister Man-in-the-Moon and stars couldn't wait to dance, out into the sky. Though they were happy that Mister Fluffy, the white cloud, wanted to help, they didn't think, it would be of any use.

"Well come on then," said Mister Sun. "Let's do it and see what happens."

Man-in-the-Moon knew well that this was not a good idea. There was no way that Fluffy white cloud could spread accross the sun and blind out Mister Sun's light. It was just going to be silly. It was all just going to be so silly.

"It's not going to work," Man-in-the-Moon shouted. "we need a darker heavier larger cloud, a cloud full of thunder and rain and storm."

Just then, a big, black cloud called Blankety-Blankety-Blanks came swishing by. "What's this all happening here?" he said to Mister Sun, "Let me try and cover you like a blanket. I am dark enough and big enough to drown out your light."

"Oh, all right then," said Mister Sun with a very grumpy face indeed.

Down below on earth, the children and animals, all over the world, were all going 'yawn, yawn, yawn' but no one could sleep. It was still too bright. Yawn, yawn, everywhere, all over the world.

Blankety-Blankety-Blanks, was just about to throw himself over Mister Sun and cover him from head to toe, all his rays too, when he heard a loud yell.

"Wait," cried Mister Sun. "I'm not ready to say goodnight yet. I'd like to stay here a little while longer. Please, oh Please."

"Well!" said Man-in-the-Moon, in a very bossy tone. "if you don't go down right now, you will be too tired to rise in the morning and the whole world will be asleep and all mixed up. No one will know, if it is night or day. It will just be all a big muddle," he cried. "Please Mister Sun, if you don't want to set, Blankety-Blankety-Blanks will cover you. We can get a selfie of me and the stars in our glory, in the night sky and show you the photo in the morning. How about that for a solution?"

At last, Mister Sun agreed. Blankety-Blankety-Blanks spread his cool, damp lining over Mister Sun. He liked the warmth of Mister Sun and Mister Sun liked his cool air, because Mister Sun, was always so hot. They snuggled together for a short while. The stars could hear yawn, yawn, coming from Mister Sun. He started to sink slowly, down behind the mountain, with the help of Blankety-Blankety-Blanks.

The sky darkened. Yawn, whispered all the boys and girls, cuddled up in their beds. Yawn, went the animals in the forest. Yawn, went the cows in the meadow. Yawn, went the deer on the hill. Yawn, went Mister Sun, as he sank deeper and deeper and deeper behind the mountain.

For a second, there was pure darkness and everything stood still. There was nothing to be seen. The whole world fell into darkness. There was not one sound. Children and animals all around the world closed their eyes, as they nodded off into dreamland.

Suddenly the moon rose high in the sky and all the stars started to twinkle and dance. It was night time again and everything went back, to being normal. The stars twinkled brightly and Man-in-the-Moon had a big smile on his face, posing for his selfie with the stars, to show Mr. Sun in the morning. He was happy again. The animals gave one last yawn, before falling into deep, sleep. The sky was very quiet and all that could be heard from down below in the world, was 'yawn', 'snore', 'yawn' and 'snore'. The majestic moon smiled down on the world and the stars twinkled in the night sky. All the children in the Land of Truth and Happiness fell fast asleep.

Would you like, if sun never went down and it was always daylight

Princess Penelope, Princess Gwen and their goblin brother, Isaac

Princess Penelope, had just turned four, and Princess Gwen, had just turned three. They were very, special girls indeed and were much loved. Their secret was, that they had wings, just like fairies and they could fly. They loved to fly on great adventures together.

I think it was on a Tuesday in November?

They were standing out in the secret garden of the Royal palace. This is where their Grandparents, Queen Rainbow and King Jack lived. The girls and their brother were spending the afternoon there. Nani was supposed to be watching them, but she fell asleep, while she was doing her knitting. Princess Penelope opened her arms and spread her beautiful wings. Princess Gwen did the same. 'Swish,' they went, as they flew towards the bright winter sky.

They flew over Rainbow Village, along the babbling river, between the trees in the forest, in and out of the caves, in the great mountain of Truth and Happiness and much further, until they arrived at Fairyland, which was right between the caves and the calm blue sea. They swooped down, waving to their fairy friends as they landed. They stayed a while and had a wonderful time, playing with their friends. They danced and sang. They tried to catch butterflies. They played hide-and-seek, between the raspberry bushes and sun flowers. They played Tag and rounders. After a while it was time to return home. They spread their wings and flew, in and out of the caves in the great Mountain of Truth and Happiness, between the trees in the forest, along the babbling river and over Rainbow Village. They swooped down and landed gently in their royal garden. The fairy princesses had a little brother called Isaac. He was, in fact, a goblin. He had turned two, on his last birthday. He looked very sad as the girls landed. Usually when they landed, he was on the swings, or sitting on a rock, painting his toe nails. But today, he was sobbing.

"I want to fly with you," he cried. "I want to fly up the bright winter sky."

"But you are a Goblin," said Gwen. "and goblins don't have wings. They cannot fly. Everyone knows this."

"But I really want to," said Isaac. "more than anything in the whole world. It's not fair." And he sobbed a while longer. He was so, so sad. His two sisters didn't want to see him upset, so they thought really hard.

Well at least Penelope did, because she was good at thinking hard and she often came up with good ideas and solutions!

"We will see if we can figure something out," she exclaimed. "You'll just have to wait here, little brother, until we get back. Come on Gwen," she said and nodded towards the sky.

With that they both opened their arms and 'swish', up they flew, up to the bright winter sky, over Rainbow Village, along the babbling river, between the trees in the forest, in and out of the caves in the great mountain of Truth and Happiness and much further until they landed in Fairyland. They called their friends to gather round. They told them about their little brother, Isaac the goblin and how desperately he wished he could fly. They asked all their fairy friends, if they had any sugestions.

"Good gracious," chanted the fairies. "Goblins can't fly" and some fairies laughed at the thought.

"But he is so sad," cried Gwen. "He truly wants to fly more than anything."

"Well," said the fairies giggling. "That is just a silliest idea we have ever heard. "Goblins flying, indeed!"

Princess Penelope and princess Gwen sighed with disappointment. They were just about to spread their wings and fly, when, kind Fairy Pink, stopped them.

"Fly over the calm, blue sea to Blue Island and speak to Fair ice Queen. She lives in a magnificent ice castle there, on Blue Mountain. The island is far out on the middle of the deep blue sea," she whispered. "She might be able to help."

Princess Penelope and princess Gwen thanked Fairy Pink, for kindly helping them. They opened their arms, spread their wings and flew back, in and out of the caves in the great Mountain of Truth and Happiness, between the trees in the forest, along the babbling river, over Rainbow Village. They swooped down, close enough to their secret garden, to tell their brother the exciting news.

"Isaac," they called. "Goblins can't fly but we are going to go to Fair ice Queen on Blue Mountain and ask if she can help you. We may be gone for some time."

"Thank you, thank you, my dear sisters," he shouted.

"No promises" yelled Penelope.

They waved goodbye to Isaac as they disappeared, up to the bright winter sky, over Rainbow Village, along the babbling river, between the trees in the forest, in and out of the caves, in the great mountain of Truth and Happiness and much further, passing over Fairyland.

"We are on the way to Fair ice Queen in her castle on Blue Mountain" they shouted down as they flew by, "to ask her help, for our goblin brother."

The fairies thought, that putting wings on a goblin, was a very crazy idea and they shouted this out to the girls in the sky. Penelope and Gwen took no notice and flew even higher. Fairy Pink waved her wand and winked at the princesses. She wished them luck on their long quest.

"I hope we find Blue Mountain before queen Rainbow finds out we're missing, or before our Nani wakes up and calls us for dinner," said Gwen.

Even though Queen Rainbow was looking after the children for the afternoon, she was in the palace preparing something delicious for dinner, so she didn't miss the children. Nani, who was supposed to watch them, was snoring away under the sycamore tree in the garden.

"We will fly until we find Fair ice Queen," replied Penelope, determined as always, to finish what she starts.

They flew for a long time over the ocean. Dolphins, who knew everything that went on in the ocean, waved to them and wished them luck on their journey.

"Look," cried princess Penelope with excitement, after a long time flying, "I see Blue Island in the distance.

Both girls were so excited, that they did not notice the angry sharks in the water, surrounding the Island.

"What are you doing flying over our ocean," cried the sharks, with a mighty roar. "We don't like strangers here, especially those with coloured wings and pretty faces and long beautiful curls," said the largest of the sharks. "Now move along, or back to where you came from."

"Don't mind him," laughed the penguins, who sat on the shore, protecting their eggs, slightly amused at what was happening. "Those sharks wouldn't hurt a fly. They don't see many strangers in these parts and when they do, they become over protective of their island, which really isn't their island. They just like to be bossy. Isn't that right?" said one of the penguins. "Leave those little girls alone! Just because you are bigger, you think you can tell everyone what to do!"

The girls were startled. Tey did not know what to say or do. So they flew around and around in circles, not knowing where to land.

"We have come to see Fair ice Queen on Blue Mountain. We want to ask her a big favour," said the girls together. They often said, the exact same sentence at the same time.

"What is the favour?" asked one of the sharks.

"You mind your own business," cried the penguin, "and let those beautiful girls get on with what they set out to do, none of your business."

"That's ok," said Princess Gwen. "It is no secret, that our goblin brother wants to fly. We are on our way, to ask Fair ice Queen, to grant him his wish."

"Maybe we should ask the queen a favour too," said the sharks, laughing and rolling in the waves. They thought it was very funny.

"Don't be silly," said the penguins. "How would that look, you, larger-than-life fish, flying in the sky?! You would frighten all the birds. That is really the silliest thing ever."

Well, the sharks thought, as they quivered in the waves. but before they could continue, they heard....

"Ahem, ahem," coughed princess Penelope. "Instead of listening to you shark and penguins having this discussion, could we possibly fly to Blue Mountain. We are expected home any minute for dinner and if we are not there, we will be in big trouble. So, if you don't mind, could we please pass?"

Just then, a group of flamingos flew by.

"Come on girls," said the flamingos. "Those penguins and sharks are always arguing over something or other. They could argue until the cows come home, about which day of the week it is. Don't mind them. They are actually very kind and gentle. We will guide you to Blue Mountain."

The girls thought it very kind of the flamingos, to offer their guidance. It was wonderful to fly, beside their beautiful, pink, elegant wings. They left the sharks and penguins and flew over Blue Island. It was a carpet of corn fields and daisies beneath them. They flew terribly high, until they came to great, big, Blue Mountain, on the far side of the Island. On the highest peak, stood the most, magnificent ice castle the girls had ever seen. It was time to fly down and land on the towered roof of the palace.

And who do you think greeted the girls on their landing? There was a grand, old duke, standing proudly in his red uniform and his blue sash. He was surprised to see two, beautiful princesses, land on the roof of the ice castle.

"What a pleasure," he said. "What can I do for you lovely girls?"

"We need to see Fair ice Queen," they said, "to ask if she can give us wings for our goblin brother."

"Seriously, wings for a goblin! I've never seen a goblin fly and I don't think I will ever see such a sight, but you may see Fair ice Queen. She doesn't get many visitors. I believe she will be happy, to see you two beautiful girls."

He turned on his heels and beckoned the girls to follow him. They walked along a stone corridor, down a winding staircase, through a room of pink screw-drivers, down a narrow staircase made of solid gold steps, through a room of flowers, a room filled with toffee apples, a room of chocolate cakes, a room of mirrors and into a huge hall with walls of jewels, jellybeans and sticker books.

In the centre of that room, was a great throne, made of pink feathers and upon it, sat the most beautiful lady the girls had ever seen. She had the longest, red hair and wore a gown of pink and purple. Her crown had a million sparkles.

They explained their wish to the queen, while eating jelly beans.

"I have never been asked for such a wish," said the queen after they had told her the story about their brother and the fairies.. She paused for a moment. She looked at these two beautiful girls and saw that they were truly sad.

"Oh, please dear Fair ice Queen," begged Penelope and Gwen together, with their mouths full of yummy jelly beans. "Our little brother is so sad and we do want him to fly with us. We miss him, when we go on our adventures. Please?"

The queen, reached behind her diamond, studded throne into a basket of bubbles. She looked up towards the ceiling, that was decorated with oranges bananas and berries and said a few magic words. She reached deep into the bubbles. She pulled out a bicycle.

"No, that won't do," she said. She then pulled out a parachute, an aeroplane, a sponge thingamajig, a pair of green fluffy boots, two white rabbits, a ball of yellow wool, three butterflies and at last, a pair of blue wings. The girls' faces lit up as they witnessed this magic.

"Here you are. That's the first time, I have ever pulled anything out of those bubbles. I must get the grand old duke to repair the bubbler, so that it works easier next time, if there is a next time. I don't get any visitors here. I am too far out at sea. You are my first visitors and you are kind sisters indeed, taking care of your little brother. Because of this, I will grant your wish and give you these wings. I have one condition though."

The girls waited.

"When you travel on your adventures, you are to look out for stray or hurt animals in the forest and in the waters. You may then take them home and help them to recover. When they have recovered, you can set them out into the wild again. May I ask that of you?"

The girls agreed. They were giddy with excitement. They loved animals and they were prepared to help any animal in need.

"And you may come back to visit me sometime and tell me of your wonderful, caring work.

The girls both nodded in agreement. Their mouths were still full of jelly beans. Fair ice Queen beckoned them to follow. She walked with them along walls of jewels, sticker books and jellybeans, into a large hall, back through a room of crystals, a room of chocolate buttons, a candy floss room and a room of jigsaw puzzles. They walked up a pink fluffy staircase, along a corridor of silver rabbits, and back out on to the highest point on the castle tower.

"Thank you so much, Fair ice Queen," cried both girls, as they stood on the castle ledge and prepared to fly. They both held the blue wings, for their little brother. The girls waved to the grand old duke, as they flew high above the palace and across Blue Island. They then flew out into the big calm ocean, waving to the dolphins as they passed. The penguins and sharks, were still arguing over something. They all stopped briefly, to wave the girls on their way and then continued their discussion. The pink flamingos joined them, as they all flew together, back to the Land of Truth and Happiness. As they passed Fairyland, the flamingos flew back to their home, wishing the girls the best of luck. The girls called down to the fairies, to let them know they had wings for their little brother. The fairies waved and cheered with good wishes.

Penelope and Gwen continued to fly, through the caves, in the great mountain of Truth and Happiness, between the trees in the forest, along the babbling river, over Rainbow Village, until they reached the royal garden, hoping to be there in time for dinner. Isaac was asleep in the bright sunshine. The girls crept up beside him. They called him quietly and waited for him to wake.

"Look" they said, "Look at what Fair ice Queen gave us for you."

Isaac's eyes lit up. He was so happy when he saw the wings.

"They look wonderful," he said with great joy.

"Let's fly," said princess Gwen and princess Penelope. They opened their arms, spread their wings and took to the bright winter sky.

"Come on Isaac," the girls called out. "Come and fly with us. It's easy now that you have your own wings. Come on now, let's fly."

Isaac ran along the garden, like a little duckling learning to fly. Nothing happened. He could not fly.

"Come on Isaac," shouted Penelope. "You can do it. I know you can, because you are so brave. Try again."

It was a very difficult at first but on the third attempt, Isaac ran along the garden path, opened his arms, spread his brand, new, blue wings and up he went to join his sisters. It was much better than Isaac could have imagined. The three were so happy, flying around together. After a short while, they heard their Nani call them for dinner.

"Come on children, Queen Rainbow has made your favourite dinner of Pizza and apple slices."

"Just in the nick of time," said Penelope. "And I am so hungry from all that flying around today."

From that day on, the siblings flew up to the blue sky, over Rainbow Village, along the babbling river, between the trees in the forest, through the caves in the great Mountain of Truth and Happiness and much further. Sometimes they stopped at Fairyland. Other times they went on wonderful adventures out over the calm, deep, blue sea and visited the penguins and sharks. They flew with the flamingos. The visited Fair ice Queen on Blue Mountain at least once a month. They felt free when they were flying. They loved helping and saving animals from dangerous circumstances. They became super heroes, among their animal friends, in the Land of Truth and Happiness.

If you had wings, where would you like to fly?

Princess Penelope's visit to doctor Brian

One fine day, princess Penelope and princess Gwen got up early to play outside in the royal garden. It was a beautiful spring day. The garden was layered with flowers of many colours. They were blue, purple, yellow, orange and violet

I think it was on a Sunday in April?

Penelope, aged four, and Gwen, aged three, wanted to show mommy how high they could jump, on the trampoline. They had been practising with their Nani, during the week. It was a very sunny day. There were so many shapes in the fluffy white clouds in the sky.

"It's a good day for looking at clouds," said Gwen.

Mommy, countess Kasey, and Penelope both agreed. Yes it is a good day for looking at clouds and finding shapes of animals. Mommy added, "remember we are going to see your grandmother, queen Rainbow for lunch. We will meet all your cousins, so we can‚t stay too long on the trampoline. Ok girls?"

"Of course, mommy," they both agreed. The girls loved to meet and play with their cousins.

They wore pretty, sun dresses, leggings and wellies, and needless to say, they had their sun protection cream on. They climbed the long path to their secret play garden, which was way, up, behind the castle, checking the newly planted seeds on the way. Some of the seeds had started to peep above the earth, showing little green heads. The girls planted them with Nani, about three weeks previous and they liked to watch the transformation, from seed to flower. They checked the progress every other day.

They turned right, just before the fairy garden, through the tall trees, into the play area. First, they sat on the swings. They could swing so high, that they could see over the trees and down to the valley, to where their royal cousins lived. They could see dolphins, jump in the lake. Then they kicked off their royal wellies, climbed up the ladder to the trampoline and started to jump around. They ran and played together, sometimes holding hands. And they sang about being sisters and *best friends doing everything together.* They did star jumps and laughed heartily, having so much fun. They jumped and tumbled for a long time. They were getting a little tired.

"Look how high we can jump mommy!" said Penelope as she sprung from the trampoline, tucking her knees to her belly and almost reached the sky.

Gwen, who was very little, suggested that they lay down and look at the shapes in the clouds, for a while.

"I see a rabbit," said Penelope.

"Yes, so do I," replied Gwen, I also see a little puppy."

"Me too," said Mom. "And I see a puppy with big ears."

They were having such fun, pointing out all the shapes in the fluffy white clouds.

"It must be very windy up in the sky," whispered Gwen. "Those clouds are moving very fast."

They loved to look at how the formations appeared in the clouds.

"Let's jump again," said both girls as they got to their feet and jumped even higher.

"Just a few more minutes now, You have done a lot of jumping today. You are getting tired and one of you might get hurt."

"Ok mommy," replied the children.

The girls knew they only had a few, more minutes to jump, so they began to dance and twirl and tumble and cartwheel very quickly. They laughed and bounced, as high as they could. They landed on their bums and then back to their feet. They hopped and ran and laughed even more. They were having the best time.

Suddenly Penelope missed her footing and tumbled on her side, landing on her left elbow. She cried out in pain! Mommy, who had been standing outside the trampoline on the grass, quickly rushed to the side of her daughter. She cuddled her as she always did, when one of the children hurt themselves.

"Where does it hurt, my darling?" she asked.

"Ow, my elbow hurts. I can't move my arm. It hurts too much," cried Penelope, with tears rolling down her cheeks.

Mommy took Penelope in her arms and carried her down home, with Gwen following closely behind.

Daddy, earl Matthew, who was playing games with their little brother, ran to the door when he heard all the commotion. Daddy gave his daughter a big hug and then strapped her arm with a tea towel and let her rest in his arms, until she fell asleep.

After a short sleep, she didn't feel well. Her arm hurt. She could not lift or move her forearm. Mommy decided there and then, that it would be wise to bring her to the hospital emergency room, to let doctor, Brian, take a look at her arm.

Daddy, Gwen and their little brother, Isaac, drove to Queen Rainbow's palace, where all the cousins were meeting, for Sunday lunch.

Mommy and Penelope drove to the hospital. They had to wait in the hospital waiting room, a while, before Doctor Brian came to check her arm.

First of all, Doctor Brian admired Penelope's pretty, purple dress and sparkling crown. While Doctor Brian was checking princess Penelope's pulse, he asked her name and age.

"Mm, you are very brave for a little girl of only four years," he remarked when she answered. "This little arm needs to have an X-ray," he said. "I have to see how it is on the inside, under your skin and check if there is a broken bone."

"I know all about X-rays," Penelope said, to Doctor Brian's surprise. "I learned all about how they work, in my first aid day in pre-school and Daddy is teaching me all about paramedics and ambulances."

"Well that's just fantastic. You surely know then, that you must remove your crown and your bracelets when going into the x-ray room. Your jewels will get in the way of the image and make the X-ray look all wrong."

She handed her crown to Mommy and her bracelets to the nice nurse, Martin. She was a little anxious. Mommy gave her a big hug and told her that it would only take five seconds and that it wouldn't even hurt one bit. Doctor Brian added that she would get a special X-ray star, afterwards for being a brave patient. That put a smile on her face. She had to sit on a high chair. A big funny-looking camera came down from the ceiling and stopped just in front of her arm. She stayed very still, until the radiologist was finished taking a photo.

"It didn't hurt one bit," she said with great excitement, when the radiologist had finished.

It was all over in a few minutes. Doctor Brian, looked very thoroughly at the X-ray pictures. He said that there were no broken bones, but he thought, that her elbow had a nasty sprain and he put a sling on Penelope's arm, to keep it from moving too much. She was very happy with her sling. She wanted to show her sister and brother and all her cousins. Mommy called queen Rainbow and asked her to let everyone know, that Penelope was alright. She had a nasty sprain in her arm and she has a sling. Mommy said they would leave the hospital soon and would join the family for Sunday lunch and maybe a treat.

Penelope's siblings and cousins couldn't wait to see the sling on her arm. They thought it was so cool to have only one arm to use. She would get everything she wanted. She would get lots of ice-cream, they were sure of it. They wanted to hear all about Doctor Brian and the X-ray machine.

Penelope, had to keep her arm very still for a couple of days, so that it could heal and become strong again. Nani knit her a blue Teddy with a sling on his arm, just like hers. And in just a few days, her arm felt much better. One week later, Nani brought Penelope back to the hospital, to see Doctor Brian. Her arm was healing really well. He asked if she was strong enough to remove the sling.

"Yes," she said with a big smile. She longed to move her arm freely again and most of all, she wanted to jump high on the trampoline.

"You can jump, but only very gentle, on the trampoline," said Doctor Brian

Penelope was very happy with this news from Doctor Brian, though she didn't have much energy. Having a hurt arm was not really much fun. She just wanted a big cuddle from mommy and daddy and to go home and be with her little sister and brother.

Have you ever fell and hurt yourself. Did you have to visit the doctor?

Princess Zoe Meets Henry Rabbit

Princess Zoe had no one to play with,in the Richmond residence. Her little brother, prince Evan, was sleeping. Her older brother, Prince Alex was at rugby training with daddy, baron Michael. It was no fun being at home with no one to play with. Mom, baroness Caroline, was very busy with the housework. She didn't have time to play or read or do anything.

I think it was on a Monday in March?

Princess Zoe longed to go out in the royal garden and play, even though it had been raining and the wind had been howling all night and everything in the garden was just soaking wet. This morning the grass was greener and the flower beds were wet and muddy. There were lovely muddy puddles everywhere. All the playthings in the royal playground were drenched.

"Please mom, can I go out just for a while? I'll just walk around and stay nice and clean. I can look at the flowers and listen to Robin redbreast sing."

The rain had stopped and the sun was starting to peek through the clouds. Zoe, knew that the bees and butterflies would be flying from flower to flower, during the sunny spell

Mom Caroline thought for a minute. "Just for a little while then, until prince Evan wakes up from his nap and don't you go splashing in those muddy puddles with your pretty dress and your new sandals." Mom knew quite well, that the first thing Zoe was going to do, was splash in the little puddles.

"Try to stay clean for tea," said Mom. Daddy and your brother will return in twenty minutes."

"Twenty minutes," Princess Zoe said. "Is that more than one hour or is it just a little while?"

"That's just enough time for you, not to get up to much mischief," mom replied. "And definitely not enough time for you to soil your lovely new yellow dress."

"Is it more than a half hour?"

"You never mind how long it is, just make sure you stay clean and don't get up to any mischief. I will call you very soon for tea."

Zoe went into the royal garden and admired the flowers. She could see Robin redbreast sitting way up high in a tree. She said hello and walked for a short time. She chatted to herself and chatted to the colourful butterflies and bees. She was just about to splash in the first puddle she found, when she spotted, right in front of her, a rabbit.

"What are you doing out in this terrible wet weather" asked the rabbit, "and why don't you have your welly boots on? You can't go splashing in muddy puddles with sandals. Did your mom not tell you?"

"Well, I never," said Zoe. "I've never in my life seen such a thing! a cheeky rabbit standing there right in front of me, asking me all kinds of questions. If you want to know, I was bored." She went on to explain that everyone at home were either asleep or busy and she had no one to play with.

"Mm," mumbled the rabbit. "Would you like to go on a little adventure with me? Then you won't be bored anymore."

"No, never," replied Zoe. "You are a stranger. I have just met you. I don't even know your name, or where you come from, or what on earth your'e doing here in our beautiful garden, asking too many questions. You are very curious. I suppose you are just digging holes and making a mess?"

"Well, excuse me your ladyship," said the rabbit, bowing down before Zoe. "I do beg your royal pardon, but I actually live here and my father before me and his father before him all lived here, on exactly this spot. We were living on these grounds, even before it was your royal home, so I think that makes me royal also. And my name is Henry, for your information."

"Is that really true?" asked Zoe. "I happen to be Princess Zoe but you can call me Zoe. You may well be Royal but where do you live, I don't see any rabbit castle around here and I know this garden pretty well."

"My home, ahem, I mean my castle, is under the earth. I have to travel down a hole in the ground, to get to it," said Henry. "I can take you there, to meet my rabbit family. It is a magical place, where there are no clocks and no time. Once you travel underground, time stands still. You can stay one hour or one day. Time never moves on when you are there. Time will stand still and you won't even be missed by your mother."

"If time never moves on, then how can you get old in Rabbit World?" asked Zoe.

"That's a tricky one," replied Henry. You see we only get older when we come above ground and we love to come up and play, in your wonderful garden, for your information."

"Are you tricking me?" asked Zoe curiously, "My mom always calls me every ten minutes to check if I am ok. Does time really stand still under the earth?"

"Yes" replied Henry, "hand on my heart," he said, placing his front paw on his chest. It's the very truth and my wife and two boys will be very happy to have a visitor. We don't get many down in those parts."

"Ok," replied Zoe. "Just because you are a rabbit and you do live on this ground, or under this ground. Yes, I will go with you, only for ten minutes. What about my pretty dress? Will it be very muddy down there?"

"Well, just a little, while we are travelling down," said Henry. "But my castle is spotlessly clean. You don't have to worry about getting dirty there. My wife is always tidying and making the place beautiful, with flowers and new curtains and lots of nice things."

"Great," Zoe said. "I will just have one look around the garden, to make sure Mom is not looking for me and we can be on our way."

Henry lifted a big, green, patch of grass from near the rose bed and sure enough there was a big hole, big enough for Zoe to climb down. There were seven steps leading down to the entrance of Henry's castle. To tell the truth, it didn't look very much like an entrance to a castle, but Grandma Rainbow always says, that one's home is one's castle, so Zoe supposed that Henry was right in believing that this, is his castle.

Henry went first and Zoe followed. It was quite dark in the long passage. Zoe was a little frightened. Then Henry lit a torch.

"Can you see me?" he shouted back to Zoe.

"Yes," she replied. "I can follow you very easy, because I can hear you and I can see you very well. But please don't go too far ahead or I'll be scared."

"I hear you," Henry said. "We are nearly there. I just need to whistle a secret code, to let my family know that we are on the way. They will then open the door. We don't want intruders."

After a long journey, they came to a tiny house, with a pink door. On the window sills, stood baskets, overflowing with many beautiful flowers. Henry whistled again and the door swung open. A lady rabbit threw her arms around him, saying how much she had missed him. Then she smiled at princess Zoe.

"My goodness," said Mrs Rabbit. "Do we have the honour of having a real princess to join us for tea."

"Wel, am, yes, Mrs. Rabbit," said Zoe very quietly. How do you know I am a princess?"

"Oh, call me Ruby," said Mrs Rabbit. "because that is my name and you are so familiar to me. I know you because I watch you playing up in the garden, with your two brothers. The little one is prince Evan and the big boy is prince Alex. He kicks the rugby ball very hard around the garden, so we need to be careful when he is about. My two boys spend a lot of time running around your royal garden, playing hide and seek with you and your family, even though you don't even notice. It's the most fun when your cousins come to visit and the garden is full of people. We run around in the grass and through the flower beds and when one of your royal family comes along, we hide very quickly. It's great fun. We also go on the royal swings and slides when you're not about and we collect flowers to decorate our front door and we dig up carrots from your garden. You see those flowers there on our windows!"

"Ok Ruby," said Henry. "That's enough information now. I don't think Zoe wants to hear about all the mischief we get up to in their garden. Let us all have some tea and your freshly baked apple pie."

"I don't drink tea," whispered Zoe to Henry, with her hand half covering her mouth.

"Of course, you do," he replied. "Everyone drinks tea, especially my Ruby's tea. It is made from wild berries and it tastes delicious. These are my two boys," he said, pointing at the twin boys, who had just sat down.

"Roger and Robbie, please say a nice hello to our visitor."

They just giggled shyly. They were not used to visitors, especially one as beautiful as Princess Zoe and with such a pretty dress, although it is a little dirty. They smiled shyly at her and patted the empty chair between them, beckoning her to come and join them.

They all sat and had tea and cake. They told each other funny rabbit stories of how they lived down under the ground and how they had to steer clear of foxes. Zoe told them stories about her over-ground world and about her life and family.

"My big brother, Alex," she told them, "is a great scholar and a great Rugby player and I'm going to play rugby, also, as soon as I turned six. Mommy said I could and when I get very big, I'm going to be a pharmacist, like my mom. My little brother, is always getting up to mischief, but he is so cute and we all love him so much," she continued.

It was so charming, being here with family Rabbit. Ruby was a perfect host, making sure that Zoe's cup was never empty and her plate always filled with yummy apple pie and ice cream. Zoe was having the best fun ever.

Zoe wished that her cousins, princesses Lola, Penelope and Gwen were there. I bet they won't believe me, when I tell them about my big adventure, with the rabbit family.

The five of them chatted, for a long time and they did a fifty-piece puzzle together. It seemed like a very, long time had passed. Zoe was getting a little anxious.

"I had better be getting back home," said Zoe at last. "I am feeling a little tired from all this travelling and all this yummy cake." She thanked the family, for their kindness and hospitality. She gave them a big hug and waved goodbye.

"You can call anytime," said Ruby. "and bring your cousins, if you like but not too many at one time, as you see our house, I mean our castle, is very little."

"Thank you again," replied Zoe. "Maybe you could come and visit me too. Our castle is so big that our parents will ever know you are there."

And with that they waved each other good bye. They were all best friends now and looked forward to seeing each other again. Henry guided Zoe up the rabbit hole, back to the royal garden. He kissed her on the cheek and gave her a big hug. They were sad saying goodbye to each other. She walked around for a little while, thinking about her new friends under the ground, until she heard her mom calling her name.

"Zoe, Zoe, it's time to come on in now. Tea is ready and I have baked delicious apple pie."

"Oh no", whispered Zoe to herself. "I'm sure I'm in trouble for being gone for so long and if I eat one more piece of apple pie, I will surely burst. I just cannot fit any more pie in my tummy."

She strolled very slowly, over to the open door. Usually, if she heard the word pie, she ran home with excitement, but not today.

When she reached the door, she realised that her crown was missing. (But that's another story.) Mom was waiting with a smiling face. Her smile soon turned to frown when she saw the mud on her daughter's beautiful dress and her hair all messed up.

"What on earth were you doing out there, Zoe, you look like you have been rolling in mud for hours and you've only been gone for ten minutes. My goodness, I have never seen you in such a state. Your dress is ruined."

"But Mommy, I had the most wonderful time. I went down to Henry Rabbit's castle, under the ground. They had flowers from our garden. I met his lovely family. There was his wife, Ruby, and his two sons, Roger and Robbie, and we ate apple pie and drank lots of special tea, and I was there for hours but time stands still there, so it only seems like ten minutes to you, mommy."

"What on earth are you talking about, Zoe? What is that nonsense about, I never heard the like of it before. How can you fit down a rabbit hole? And as for eating apple pie and drinking tea, tea" she repeated. "Actually, you were only out for ten minutes. So how can you explain all that? You are just making up a story so that I will not scold you for being so dirty."

It didn't matter how Zoe tried to explain, her Mom was never going to believe her. Mom brought her in and gave her a nice warm bath. Her dad and prince Alex arrived home. Little Evan woke and they all sat down to tea. Zoe could not eat one piece of apple pie. Daddy remarked that it was very odd, that his daughter did not wish to eat cake and that maybe princess Zoe was poorly.

"No, she is not poorly," said Mom. "She has a great imagination though and she can truly make up the best fairy tales. Tea, apple pie and a castle in a rabbit hole, indeed. What a fairy tale!"

Prince Alex looked at Zoe. He knew there was more to her story. He would hear about it later. Zoe couldn't eat mom's apple pie but she thought about Ruby's apple pie and the wonderful afternoon she spent, under the ground with Henry in his rabbit hole. She couldn't wait for her cousins to have a sleep over, at her house. She would tell them about her fantastic, underground adventure. Maybe they would like to meet Henry Rabbit and his family or Henry and his family might like to come up to her house and visit them. She just knew that it was true, that she was down a rabbit hole drinking tea and eating apple pie.

Or was it all a dream? What do you think?

Princess Lola's First Gymnastic Performance

It was a very exciting day in Ashford Manor. Princess Lola was six years old and today was the day of her first, ever, gymnastics performance. Lola loved writing, drawing and swimming but most of all she loved gymnastics and she was very good, even though she had only started lessons, four months ago. Lola was going to perform at her gymnastics club. She was feeling lots of butterflies in her tummy. She was very excited.

I think it was on a Thursday in May?

She was so good at gymnastics, that she was the only first grader, to be chosen, to perform with the 2nd and 3rd graders. After Lola returned home from school, mommy bathed her and wrapped her in her cosy robe to dry. Daddy had to go away on business for the day and was not sure if he would be back on time, to see his little princess perform. He was not happy about this, but sometimes even a Lord cannot get out of doing his jobs. He wished his daughter the best of luck, before she left for school that morning and drove off. To make princess Lola feel more comfortable and supported, mommy called queen Rainbow and asked if she and king Jack, would like to come and watch the performance.

"Yes," said queen Rainbow with great enthusiasm. "There is nothing we would like to do more, than see our darling grandchild display her talent and hard work."

"Ok," said Mommy, "we will send the royal carriage to collect you both at five thirty. The performance starts at six."

"Perfect" replied queen Rainbow, "I am looking forward and I'm certain that king Jack will be thrilled. Will Princess Lola's little brother, prince Noah, also be there?"

"Yes" Mommy replied. "We will all be there, except Daddy. He is out of town on business. Such a shame! Lola is very disappointed but we cannot change that now. He'll try his best, to be back before the performance commences."

Queen Rainbow was delighted to be included. She just loved to take part in her grandchildren's lives. "See you all later then," said queen Rainbow.

"When I'm six I'm going to do gymnastics too," said little prince Noah. He was very proud of his big sister and he wanted to do everything she did, even wear nail varnish, but only on his toe nails.

Lola was upset at the thought of daddy not being home. She cheered up though when mommy told her, that her grandparents, the queen and king, would be there to support her.

Mom dressed Lola in her beautiful, red leotard that Nani bought her for Christmas. She tied Lola's long, curly hair in a ponytail. She packed some drinks and an extra hair tie, just in case, one fell off. After 5 o'clock, Mom got the children to sit in the car. She checked that the safety belts were clicked in properly. She gave each of them a bottle of water and drove along the poppy fields, through the valley into Rainbow village to the venue.

Prince Noah sang two songs on the way. He sang, the one about the seven continents. He loved to sing.

Continents, continents, do you know your continents?

North, south, east, west, all around the world..." and so on.

The other song was similar but it was about planets. He sang very loud and mom joined in.

"Planets, planets, do you know your planets?

Mars and Jupiter and Mercury..."

He loved to sing. He sang every time he was going somewhere in the car. Lola didn't sing. She was nervous and excited. All she could think of was her performance and she missed her daddy.

Mom and the children arrived at the venue, just ten minutes before six. Queen Rainbow and king Jack were already there. They drove in the royal carriage and arrived at the venue, in plenty of time. They secured the best seats for the rest of the family, in the very front row, so that they'd have a perfect view, of the whole performance. Princess Lola was very happy to see her grandma. She loved when queen Rainbow and grandad came to see her perform. They attended the Christmas pageant in school, Grandparents' day and Lola's swimming competition. Lola was equally, excited and anxious. She had a pain in her tummy.

"That's just nerves," said queen Rainbow, "maybe you just need to go to the toilet, before the performance."

Lola agreed and went to the bathroom. She always needed to, before something exciting, like the cinema or going on a long drive, or going to the Park or the Beach. Afterwards she felt much better. It probably was all the excitement. All of a sudden, she was a little unsure of herself.

All the performing children were called to assemble by the instructors. Lola was feeling very nervous and still so disappointed, that daddy Jesse could not be there.

The children, from the ages of four to fourteen, lined up to start. The sports hall was prepared, with different excercise stations. There were parallel bars, uneven bars, balance beam, pommel horse and mats for floor work. All the seats were filled except daddy's seat. Mom and queen Rainbow were worried, that Princess Lola would lose her nerve and decide not to take part. But Lola waved out to them from the performing area, with a smile on her face, an extra special smile actually. She looked very happy and not even one bit nervous. Mom felt better now. She was so proud of her little girl.

The children performed different disciplines. Lola was full of confidence. She danced and jumped, tumbled, and balanced. She did her performance on the high beam, without a shiver or a shake and landed with precision. She was fantastic. There was huge applause from all the parents, so proud of their little girls and boys. Queen Rainbow, mom, king Jack and little prince Noah gave Lola a standing ovation. They were so proud of their little princess. She did all that, even without Daddy being there to cheer her on.

Lola smiled and waved to them, after doing the best, gymnastic performance ever. She then waved to the back of the hall, with an extra special smile and she blew a kiss. Her family wondered, to whom was she blowing a kiss.

They turned around only to see daddy, standing there as proud as any daddy could be. He had been there for the whole performance. He stayed at the back of the hall throughout the performance, because he did not want to walk to his seat and disturb the view, for all the other parents. He arrived just before it all started. He saw Lola tumble and jump and cartwheel and everything else. He blew mom a kiss and waved to the others. No wonder princess Lola was so happy and confident, during the show. She had spotted her daddy, from the very beginning. That's why she was so confident. All her family were there to see her in her first ever gymnastic display. She received a great big shiny medal. She got her photo taken with all her team mates. She got the biggest hugs from daddy, mom, her grandparents and even Noah.

Afterwards Daddy treated the whole family, to ice cream of their choice. It was a wonderful day. Lola was very pleased, at how she had performed. They all sang in the car on the way home, even Lola.

Wll we sing a song together now. Maybe your favorite song?

Billy, Brian and Bobby. Goldfish on their Journey

Queen Rainbow's eight royal grandchildren, came to visit one day. They are Penelope, Lola, Evan, Alex, Zoe, Isaac, Noah and Gwen. Now if you take the first letter of all those names, it will spell the word 'Pleazing' and I'll tell you, queen Rainbow was always very pleased to see them. The children couldn't go out and play in the royal garden, because it was raining too heavy. It had been raining all night and all morning. It was the worst rainy day ever. They sat around the big fire, eating crackers. Nani told them a great story, about the rainy day she remembered, when she was a little girl. It was the day that the little family of goldfish that lived in a lake on the top of Keeper hill, had to swim for their lives and were washed into the big ocean.

I think it was on a Sunday in April?

Daddy Goldfish, Mommy Goldfish and three boys called Billy, Bobby and Brian, lived happily on the top of the hill in a great green lake. They swam and ate insects. They were so high on the hill, that they could see above the trees and down into the valley. On this particular day, there was a rainstorm, the biggest rainstorm that Family Goldfish had ever lived through.

Rain spilled down so heavy, that the water in the lake, began to rise. It rose all night and all day. The lake overflowed. The water had nowhere to go, only down Keeper hill, across the valley and towards the ocean. The water poured out, taking with it, some flowers and pebbles and, the goldfish family. One by one, the Goldfish were washed out of the lake, first Mommy, then Daddy, then their three boys. They were forced out against their will. They had to swim for their lives, tumbling and rolling and crashing down the hillside, in the strong flow of water. The children cried out to their parents to help them. They were very frightened. They could hear their mommy shouting, at the top of her voice.

"Stay together, children," Mommy fish warned, as her baby, boys tossed and turned in the strong current. "Don't lose sight of Mommy and Daddy boys, and whatever you do, don't lose sight of each other."

"Hold on boys and try to swim," instructed Daddy Fish, with much determination and much worry. He wanted to say more but, before he could, a strong gush of water pushed him and mommy out of the lake and down the hillside. They were separated from their children.

They were both frantic with worry. The boys were still very little. They had never been out of the lake on Keeper Hill before. They could not possibly swim against such a strong current. They cried out to the boys, again and again. They were beginning to lose sight of the boys, but before they were washed down the hillside, Mommy shouted very loud.

"Head towards the ocean. We will be waiting there for you, no matter how long it takes. Bobby, Brian and Billy. Mommy and daddy love you very much." And then they were gone.

"Mommy, Daddy, where are you? We are alone," Bobby cried. The other two boys were too frightened to speak.

There was just the sound of the wind in the trees and the gushing of water, that now looked like a great, long river, flowing down Keeper hill, down and down and down into the big blue sea, or the ocean as the adults called it. They had never been the ocean. They just heard about it from their story books and they could see it from the lake, on the mountain, where they lived. The boys held on to each other's fins and swam as fast as they could, until they came to a big muddy puddle where they stopped for a rest. Their tiny hearts were pounding. They were afraid of never finding their parents again.

They rested in the muddy puddle for a while. Bobby spotted a fluffy dog standing quite near the edge.

"Hey Mr dog," he yelled. "Have you by any chance seen two big goldfish, swimming by?"

"Woof, woof", barked the dog, "Yes I saw two fish, not exactly swimming. They were being tossed and turned, with the strong flow of water, down the hill towards the big ocean. They were very panicky. I could understand what they were saying. They kept repeating three names. Yes, the names were Billy, Bobby and Brian, I think. It was very hard to hear, with the sound of the wind and the rapid flowing water, but with my keen sense of hearing, I could hear them very clear."

"Thank you, Mr dog," Bobby said. He then called his brothers and told them what Mr dog had said. Off they went swimming again, even faster this time.

They had to hurry, if they wanted to catch Mommy and Daddy, before they got to the ocean, or they might never be re-united. The ocean is a very big place, even bigger than, Keeper Queendom.

Swimming, was hard work. They swam as fast as they could and didn't stop, until they came to another, even bigger, muddy puddle. They needed another little rest. It was not easy, trying to stay together. They were so tiny and the water was moving rapidly. But, up to now, they were doing well. Even though it was scary, they looked out for each other, like siblings do.

Billy noticed a big shadow, above the water's surface. He was very curious. He rustled up the courage, to pop his head out of the water, for a peek. There, before his eyes, was a huge green,crocodile, just about to immerse herself into the river.

"My goodness," said Billy. "you are the largest fish I have ever seen."

"uhhh" roared the crocodile. I'm actually not a fish. I am a reptile."

"Oh, Im sorry "but please, not so loud. My ears are too tiny for loud noises."

"So sorry," said the crocodile, a little quieter, "I've never spoken to a fish, as tiny as you before. You are so tiny, just like a bug."

"I'm not that tiny," replied Billy, indignantly. "I can swim and catch flies all by myself. But I don't have time to chat. My brothers and I are looking for our mommy and daddy. We all got washed out of the lake on the mountain and now we cannot find them. Have you seen two big goldfish pass this way?"

"uhhh" she whispered, because she noticed, that Billy was blocking his ears. "I saw two tiny goldfish a while ago calling out something. I couldn't hear because they were so small and I am so large. Yes, they were swimming very quickly, in and out of the muddy puddles, down the hill, towards the ocean. The high water doesn't bother me", she went on. "I am so big and strong."

"Great," said Billy, as he swam down to his brothers. "Thank you, Miss crocodile. Have to go!" He told the boys what the Crocodile said and they set off again.

The rain softened a little and the gush of water was gentler, as they moved down the muddy mountain. They swam for what seemed like a very long time. Brian, who was the youngest, was tired of swimming so fast and he missed his parents. He started to cry. He needed a hug, a big mommy and daddy hug and a rest. The boys stopped at the next muddy puddle and sat on a big rock, right in the middle of it. Brian was so lonely for his Mommy. He was worried, that they would never find their parents. They were tired and hungry and frightened, but they did not panic.

Sometimes, on Keeper Hill, they were startled when a little girl or boy, threw a heavy rock into the lake. Mommy advised them never to panic when in danger. She told them to stay calm and quiet and everything would turn out ok. So, that is what they did. They stayed calm and quiet. The wind was dying down and they could hear the most beautiful sound. Perched high on a tree next to the muddy puddle, was a Robin, with his red breast, singing sweetly. His song was very calming for the boys, especially Brian who loved birdsong.

When he was finished, Robin redbreast looked down to the three sad goldfish below him.

"Tweet, tweet," whistled Robin redbreast. "What on earth is the matter with you goldfish. You should be glad of all this rain. You love water. You swim in water, all day long and now you can you can swim wherever you like, with all this rain. Why are you so sad?"

"We are all alone, you see. We were washed out of the lake on the top of Keeper hill and forced to swim, toward the ocean. We have lost our Mommy and and Daddy," Brian sobbed. "We are too little to see them."

"Hush little goldfish, don't be so sad," tweeted the robin. "I will fly to the top branch of the tree and look towards the ocean. Maybe I can see your parents, or see how far away the ocean is." And off he flew, to the topmost branch of the tree.

A few minutes later, he returned.

"Tweet, tweet," whistled Robin redbreast. "I didn't see your parents. They are probably too tiny under the water, but I saw the ocean. It is not so far away. You will be there in no time. There is a big ship at the ocean's edge. Maybe the captain can tell you more, about your parents. I hope you find them. Good luck on your way."

This news cheered Billy, Brian and Bobby up so much that they jumped with joy into the muddy puddle. They swam around and around with excitement before they continued their journey, even faster, down. It wasn't long, before they saw the biggest expanse of water they had ever seen. It was humongous, bigger than the world, bigger than the hill, bigger that the universe, bigger than the solar system.

"This is the ocean," said Bobby. "We are here." They were so excited and also very scared at the sight of it. They hadn't a clue what to do next.

At the ocean's edge, just as Robin explained, there was a very big ship. It was mostly white, with a big red anchor, painted on the side. The sails, reached to the clouds. The three little goldfish, felt very little indeed. They had never seen anything as big, in their lives. Robin redbreast flew overhead and reminded them, to speak to the captain. The three boys, saw the captain standing, way up on the deck.

"Hey Captain, we are looking for our mommy and daddy. Have you seen them swim by?" shouted Billy, as loud as he could.

"Ahoy, ahoy, yes I have," Captain replied. "and they told me, to watch out for three little boys and if I see them, I am to tell them, to swim under my boat and down into the deep, because that is where mommy and daddy are. Don't be afraid. Swim down under. Go on now, under as far as you can. No need to be scared."

The boys were overjoyed. "Thank you so much, Captain."

They swam under the big ship, calling Mommy and Daddy as they swam. They swam through caves and the coral and deeper. They came upon a large group of dancing fish. They had never seen so many different types of fish. There were neon fish, salmon, herring, amberjacks, snapper, bass, seahorse,sting ray, barracuda and many more. They recognised all these fish from their story books. The fish were singing and dancing and happily partying together. The boys called their mommy and daddy again and again.

Then, suddenly, they heard their names.

"Billy! Bobby! Brian!"

They followed the sounds, but all they could see were hundreds of fish, dancing and singing. There were fish everywhere. they were blue, green and rainbow. It was magical sight to behold.

We are over here, came the voices of their parents.

The dancing fish, turned around and saw the boys. They parted in the centre, to let the boys through, and there, in the middle of the dancing fish, were Mommy and Daddy. The ocean fish, were celebrating because of the two golden fish, who came to join them. They had never seen such tiny, golden fish before.

Mommy and daddy sparkled. The looked solid gold, like sunshine. They had never looked so magnificent. The boys joined them and there were hugs all around. They were all so happy to see each other. They had lots to tell each other, about their wonderful, though sometimes frightening adventure and all the animals they met along the way. The collection of fish had never seen such a beautiful golden fish family in the deep blue sea before. They danced even more and sang with joy when Mommy, Daddy, Billy, Bobby and Brian were reunited at last. And though it was a great celebration and a wonderful family reunion, Mommy, Daddy, Billy, Brian and Bobby were looking forward to going back to their lovely home, on Keeper Hill, where it was peaceful and where they could see other animals, from time to time and most of all, where they could hear Robin redbreast sing sweet song.

Have you ever been on a long trip, or to the sea, or to the zoo?

Visit to the country to see Great Uncle Gerry

It was a hot, summer day. The royal children jumped out of bed with great excitement. Penelope, Gwen and Isaac were going to visit Great uncle Gerry.

I think it was on a Thursday in July?

They were dressed in, light summer clothes. Their Nani put sun protection cream on their hands, legs and faces. Princess Penelope, even though she was sallow skinned, always remembered to apply sun cream. She did not want her skin, to burn. She said that she wanted to stay pretty, when she grew up and didn't want freckles on her face, like Nani and daddy. Princess Gwen and prince Isaac needed lots of sun cream, because they had very, pale, soft skin.

The children were very excited about this trip. They did not get to visit their Great uncle Gerry very often. Nani packed a light lunch, with plenty of fruit and water. She then checked that the children's safety belts were secure, before she drove. The children sang their favourite songs, all the way to Great uncle Gerry's. It was a long drive and many times they asked, are we there yet?"

Great uncle Gerry lived alone, far beyond Rainbow Village. He was a single man. Nani said, that, maybe didn't find the right partner, to settle down with.

Lots of adults live on their own. The children had to pass Rainbow Village and drive, for what seemed like long time, before they arrived at his big, light-blue mansion, with enormous gates and a wonderful driveway, leading to the main house. Along the driveway there were many trees, with green and purple leaves, where lots of wild animals lived. There were squirrels, rabbits, many birds, frogs, bees and foxes. If you were lucky, you might even get a glimpse of a deer or two, trying to hide behind the forestry. Gerry was a very kind and gentle man. He had wonderful garden. Part of his garden, wwas filled with beautiful flowers. The children, were never allowed to play there. He had a vegetable garden and a huge pollytunnel, behind his great big house, on the south side. This is where he grew the most wonderful vegetables and berries. The children loved to learn about vegetables growing. Gerry was the perfect teacher.

But, best of all, Gerry, had the silliest, little, white dog named Blackie, who liked to play ball and dig up the garden with his front paws.

When they arrived, Nani had to press a few buttons, before the gates opened. The children looked out the window of the car in amazement, at the long driveway and the wonderful trees. They caught a glimpse of a squirrel, running across the road and up into a tall, leafy branch. They were thrilled to be at great uncle Gerry's home and he was happy, to see the children.

Blackie, his tiny fluffy white dog, jumped for joy when he saw the children. They all walked together around the flower garden. Uncle Gerry explained, about the different kinds of flowers. He grew, pansies, roses, nasturtiums, flocks and the most wonderful mammoth sunflowers, towering to the sky.

"Trying to keep Blackie off the flowerbed is a difficult task," Gerry remarked. The children laughed at Blackie. He was very silly, even though he was getting quite old. The children's favourite part of the visit to Gerry was always the vegetable garden. They loved to see how food grew, just from a seed. Uncle Gerry brought a knife and scissors and he gave the girls, princesses Penelope and Gwen, a basket each to collect berries and vegetables, from the pollytunnel. Prince Isaac just wanted to play ball with Blackie. So off the two of them went to play. Nani went along to supervise. The girls went with great uncle Gerry.

They were very curious and wanted to know everything, about the vegetables in the polytunnel. Uncle Gerry was happy to explain everything and answer their questions. He pulled a carrot straight out of the earth in the garden. He brushed away the soil and let the girls eat it. They loved it. They had never tasted such a sweet carrot. He cut fresh kale, spinach and lettuce. He placed them in the girls' baskets. Then they went into his pollytunnel and pulled, even sweeter carrots, beetroot and tiny potatoes. Uncle Gerry explained how plants grew, how much water and heat they needed. He pulled scallions, strawberries and sweet peas and put them in the girls baskets, to take back to mommy and daddy in Sleeper-Cottage castle. While both girls were filling their baskets with vegetables, they were also filling their bellies with strawberries. Blackie came running in, all over the vegetable beds and started digging. He buried his bones in the vegetable beds. It was too funny, watching uncle Gerry trying to catch him. Before long, his beautiful, fluffy, white fur was all covered in dirt and his nose was muddy.

"Now, you see why I call him Blackie," smiled uncle Gerry.

And they all had a big laugh, looking at the dog, covering his beautiful fluffy coat, with earth.

It was time for lunch. Nani brought, freshly made vegetable soup and Uncle Gerry produced crusty, brown, bread and butter. It was delicious. All five sat down to a lovely feast of lunch. Their desert was, vanilla and strawberry ice cream. Blackie sat on the floor, with his juicy bone.

After lunch, the children said goodbye to great uncle Gerry and Blackie. They promised to return soon. All three, tired little teddies sat in their car seats, while Nani fastened their belts. Great uncle Gerry, pressed all the correct code buttons and the gates opened. Nani drove slowly, down the driveway and off home. They heard Blackie barking all the way to the gates but they were too tired to gaze out the car windows, to see if the squirrel was still sitting on his branch. After just a few minutes, the children were fast asleep. They slept all the way home. It was a great exciting and interesting day, but very exhausting, with great uncle Gerry and his funny, white dog called Blackie. The best part was watching great uncle Gerry chase after Blackie. Princess Penelope told mommy and daddy this story when they got home and they all had a great laugh.

Do you think Great Uncle Gerry enjoyed chasing Blackie?

Tinaturner and her kittens

This is a story about a clever cat, called Tinaturner who usually went on her adventures for hours at a time, or even a full day. Her owners, Annie and Jonnie never worried, because, she always returned, before dark, to her cosy basket.

I think it was a Friday in June?

Tinaturner had been missing, for one night and two days. She lived in Rainbow village with a little middle-aged woman called Annie and her husband, Jonnie. They lived in a white cottage, with a blue door. There was a pink, cast-iron gate at their entrance. Their garden was the most beautiful in the village, with millions of coloured flowers and a silver, frog waterfall, surrounded by, a family of leprechaun figurines. There were red roses, yellow gladiolus, blue cornflowers, multi-coloured pansies and white flocks, that smelled like perfume. Annie and Jonnie, were a very sweet couple. Both their children were grown up and lived elsewhere. Their daughter,Eva-Marie lived in Dublin, with her family and their son, Robbie,who is a dancer, is currently starring the new, west end production of La Cage Aux Folles. They missed the children, but their cat kept them company these days.Her name was Tinaturner but she was a handful.She was always up to mischief.

Tinaturner was with them, ever since she was a tiny kitten. She was quiet at first but she grew, into a very mischievous cat, who spent her time climbing into other people's gardens and hiding among their flowers. Jonnie had said on a few occasions that Tinaturner was too clever, running into all the gardens and getting fed by the neighbours. She used to cross the road over to the supermarket also. Jonnie was afraid that she might get knocked down by a car.

"Don't worry about her," Annie told him, on many an occasion. "I think she can take care of herself. She is loved by all the children. Everyone in the village, look out for her. She will be fine."

Annie reminded him of this, again and again.

Sometimes, Tinaturner went missing for two days at a time and then returned, with no explanation. That's what cats can do,go missing. Jonnie left the sitting room window ajar, for her, when she wandered home while they were out. He worried that she would wander off again, if she could not get into the house on her return.

It was not unusual this time, that she had been missing, well at least on the second day. But on the third day, Annie and her Jonnie got worried and went searching. The children in the village helped and so too did the kind neighbours. They searched high and low. They searched and they searched, until there was nowhere left to look. Annie and Jonnie came back home. They very sad and upset.

They worried, that they would never see their precious Tinaturner again.

Jonnie put on the kettle for a nice cup of tea and Annie sat on the sofa by the fire. Something startled her. The rug on which her armchair stood, started to move. She leapt up and screamed. Jonnie came running in, to find out what all the commotion was about. Just as he was about to ask, out from under the armchair, came their cat, with a big smile on her face and even a bigger belly. Tinaturner was pregnant!

Annie and Jonnie leapt with joy and cuddled their little cat, who would soon be a mommy. They explained to her that she would have to be extra careful, crossing roads in the future. In fact, they said, that it would be a lot safer for her to stay close to home. Tina just purred and cuddled up by the fire.

Annie took her for a walk every morning thereafter, on her lead and brought her in by the fire to rest. They did not want her wandering off, with a belly full of kittens. She stayed close to the house, most of the time. Three weeks later, she went missing from the garden. The worry started. The searching started. It went on for one whole day and night. They had almost given up, when on the morning of the second day after she went missing, Jonnie found Tinaturner in the meadow behind the back garden. She was curled into a ball, in the high green grass. First, he thought the worst and was just about to cry, when he saw teeny, tiny, little feet popping out from under Tina's belly. He was overjoyed and ran to tell Annie that Tinaturner and her three babies were safe.

"Well we must bring them home," cried Annie, as soon as she heard this wonderful news. Tinaturner is sure to be hungry and those kittens need heat and cuddles.

They brought Tina and her little family home. Annie made a cosy bed for them by the fire. There were two girls and one boy. The girls were named Cherry and Bluebell but they could not think of a name for the boy. They had never had a boy cat, so they just called him Junior, for the time being. The kittens stayed very close to their mommy for a couple of weeks, just lying beside her and getting stronger. Then the two girls, Cherry and Bluebell, started chewing Annie's knitting, Jonnie,s slippers and everything, that was close to the floor. Junior stayed quiet and close to Tinaturner. After four weeks and as they grew much bigger. They started to jump and run and hide everywhere, in the house. They climbed up the curtains, tore the good cushion covers and ruined the carpet, with their little nails.

"Oh no, look at what they have done," Annie almost cried to Jonnie one day after the kittens ripped her knitting. She was knitting a red cardigan for her granddaughter, for her fifth birthday and now it was ruined.

"We have to find homes for them," she continued. "They are just as mischievous as their mother. We will ask little Miss Mix, at the village supermarket, if we can advertise in her shop window, to find new families for them. We are getting on and we cannot run after four cats every day."

Jonnie agreed and made up a fine advertisement, with a photo of the three cute kittens and a note that said:

Our kittens

are looking for a new home.

They are adorable

They will only be given

to kind, loving families.

And with that, he marched down the road to the supermarket.

"Hello, Little Miss Mix, are you in or out?" Jonnie called in the door.

"I'm in," she replied." She was in among the shelves, sorting things. She appeared from one of the aisles, with the warmest smile you could imagine.

"What can I do for you Jonnie, on this most wonderful day?"

She called every day, a most wonderful day. She was always happy and smiling. She had red curly hair, in a bun and she always wore pretty dresses and very, cool boots.

"Could you be so kind and put a notice, on your shop window for me?" he asked, as he showed her the poster, that he was so proud of making.

She was only too pleased to help. She hoped, that the kittens would find new homes soon, so that Annie and her husband could get some quiet time for themselves, once again and Annie could finish knitting her granddaughters red cardigan, in time for her birthday.

Within three days, twenty people called to adopt the kittens. All the callers only wanted girl kittens. Two wonderful families were found for Cherry and Bluebell. They stayed for a while with Tinaturner, until they grew strong enough to leave. When they reached eight weeks, the kittens were collected, by their new families. Annie and Jonnie packed the kittens into their baskets and waved them goodbye. They were a little sad, but at the same time, they were happy not to have to tidy up every day, after the kittens ripped their house apart. They wouldn't need to search the house, high and low every evening, to find the girls before bedtime.

Later that evening, they both sat by the fire with Tinaturner and Junior, who still didn't have a name. He was growing bigger every day. They wondered, if anyone would call to adopt Junior. They decided that if no one came in the next two weeks, they would keep Junior. All four of them Annie, Jonnie, Tinaturner and Junior, sat by the cosy fire, thinking of Cherry and Bluebell. They wondered if they were nice and cosy too and if they were happy, in their new homes. They wondered also, what would become of Junior. Would he ever get a proper name. Oh! but that story is for another day.

Do you think Junior will be happy in a new home?

Junior gets a new Name

Great uncle Gerry made a very important decision one day. He lived alone and he thought he could do, with some company.

I think it was on a Friday in October.

You see, he used to have a little dog called Blackie but Blackie went to dog heaven a few months before. Gerry lived alone now, except for the spiders and mice and insects in his garden. There were foxes and deer but you wouldn't call them pets. He needed a house-pet of some kind, to keep him company. He wasn't sure if he wanted a dog, a cat or a rabbit. He lived in a big, bright, blue mansion, on a large estate, with gardens of sunflowers and vegetables. He loved gardening and he loved, when the royal children came to visit. But he was alone most of the time. His best friends all moved far away, to the Kingdom of Music in the land of the Limericks. His family were busy most of the time, with all their royal children and households.

Great uncle Gerry needed eggs and tea. He decided that, a trip to the village, was necessary. He drove, out his long driveway and along the country road, until he came, to the edge of Rainbow village. He parked his car on the first street and walked the rest of the way, to the supermarket. He liked to walk through the village and stop for a chat along the way. The first person he met was Miss Weed, the owner of the village flower shop. Miss Weed was widowed since her husband passed away, a number of years ago. When she wasn't in the flower shop, she was busy, doing her garden. She waved and said, "Hello, Gerry. It's a fine morning for weeding the garden." She always said that, even if she wasn't weeding. Sometimes, she was planting flowers or mowing the grass. All the ladies, in Rainbow Village, loved Gerry.

"It is a lovely day for weeding, Miss Weed," replied Gerry. "But your garden is so beautiful, I don't think the weeds like to grow there." And they both laughed.

Mister Lamb, the butcher, was out cleaning his shop window and looking at Sunday roasts and vegetables on display. He was ready for the weekend shoppers.

"I feel like eating roast chicken and peas for dinner. What do you think dear friend?" he asked great uncle Gerry, as he passed by. Mister Lamb loved roast. That was true, but it was also a sales pitch, for his great, home-grown, Irish meat.

"I love roast," great uncle Gerry replied. "but I also love sausages on Friday, sizzling in the pan, until they are golden brown and then, sandwiched between two slices of buttered toast."

Yummy, he thought. A nice mug of hot tea and a sausage sandwich, that's a good choice for today's dinner.

"In fact, I will buy eight sausages today," he said, as he walked into the shop with Mister Lamb. "I 'll cook them, when I get back from the supermarket." Mister Lamb loved the banter and Gerry, loved the taste of sizzling sausages.

When he arrived at the supermarket, it wasn't at all surprising, that Little Miss Mix was busy, packing shelves. As soon as he opened the door, she appeared, from behind the washing powder shelf.

"Well, she smiled. it is yourself, Gerry, and so nice to see you. What can I do for you on this most, wonderful day?"

He started to tell her, that he needed eggs and milk. They spoke about the weather, about his vegetables and her choir singing. He told her that he was thinking of getting a pet dog, or a rabbit, or a cat. Little Miss Mix's eyes lit up, as she heard this, but she was very carefully choosing her words, when she spoke "Well now, Gerry, I think that is, one of the the best ideas, you have ever had. Apart from painting your mansion bright blue and apart from growing the biggest sunflowers, I have ever seen."

"Oh, thank you, Little Miss Mix. That is very kind of you. But what kind of pet can I get? I really can't choose."

She continued. "Rabbits stay outdoor all the time. They are lovely and warm and soft, but they would never like to sit, beside your open fire. A night by the open fire would be much too warm, for a pet rabbit. Dogs are definitely a man's best friend, as you well know." They both blessed themselves and looked up towards the sky, thinking of poor little Blackie.

"They are loyal and funny Gerry, but you have to walk a dog, every day. I know you like a little walk," she said with a sweet smile. "But a dog would need to walk, at least one mile every day, even during the Sunday game."

She waited for his reaction.

"Ooaa," he frowned. "I don't know about a rabbit not liking my open fire and I don't know, about walking a dog, while the Sunday game is on the TV. Maybe I should get a cat. What about a cat, Little Miss Mix, please help me to decide?"

"Isn't it funny, that you should choose a cat Gerry and a funny coincidence, that I know of a cat, looking for a new home. He is a friendly, very well-behaved, white cat, with a black tail. At the moment, he lives with Annie and Jonnie down the street. Isn't that a peculiar coincidence? Why don't you call by, on your way home? I will phone ahead and tell them, that you're on your way."

"I can't thank you enough Little Miss Mix." Gerry, paid for his eggs and tea and went on his way, to visit Annie and Jonnie in their cottage.

When he arrived, they were both standing at the front door smiling. Annie was holding Junior, the cat, in her arms.

"This is he," she said, with great enthusiasm. "He is the most wonderful calm cat, not like his two, wild, mischievous sisters. He likes to cuddle up in front of the fire. We have Tinaturner, a long time. One pet in this house, is enough for us to manage. We have grown very attached to Junior, but we know that you, Gerry, will give him a good home. His two sisters have very, nice, new homes. Most people only wanted girls. The few who wanted a boy, did not please us too much. On the other hand, you, Gerry, are the perfect adoptive parent, for Junior and maybe you could give him a real name. We couldn't think of any to suit him."

Great uncle Gerry was overwhelmed with excitement, as he gently took Junior into his arms. This was definitely the best pet for him. Junior will love to sit beside the fire and there would be no need to walk him, during the Sunday Game.

Gerry thanked them both. He told them that they, and Tinaturner, are always welcome to visit his home, to see Junior. They were all very pleased with this outcome, especially great uncle Gerry, who lived alone. He had just received his very own pet and two new people-friends.

It was a cold November evening, a few weeks after Gerry brought Junior home. They both sat by the fire. Gerry on the sofa and Junior curled beside him, on a cushion. Great uncle Gerry got very ill. He felt a pain in his chest and couldn't breathe properly. He called Doctor Brian and explained. An ambulance was arranged, to bring Gerry to hospital. He had a heart attack. He had to stay in hospital, for four days. During this time, Annie fed junior and checked in on him, every day . She made sure he was cosy, wrapped in his basket. She did not light the fire, in case Junior would burn himself. She made his basket very cosy, with extra blankets. But Junior was so used to the fire each night, that he was not as cozy, as usual.

On the fourth day, on Gerry's return, Junior heard a familiar car, in the drive. With so much excitement, he ran out the open door, just as Great uncle Gerry was entering. Gerry didn't notice Junior running past him. He went into the house, locked the door and went straight to bed. He wasn't feeling so well and he needed to lie down. Junior was left outside in the cold. He was alone. He smelt the familiar diesel engine in Gerry's car and crawled up inside, to heat himself. He stayed there for a very long time, even when the engine cooled down. He was cold and scared, but he did not move. He stayed where he was, all night long. When the engine finally fired up and made a terrible noise, he did not move. When the car moved along the road, he did not move. When the car stopped at the red traffic lights, he did not move. Even when the car came to a standstill, he didn't dare move. Gerry arrived at Annie's and Jonnies house. Junior was too scared to move, in case the engine would eat him up. He sat there very quietly, when the engine went quiet and listened to the voices.

"Junior is missing, we have to find him," cried great uncle Gerry.

"But I fed him and made sure he was cosy," replied Annie with a big smile. Are you sure, you checked everywhere in the house. Did you search the cupboards, under the rug, in his basket, under your bed, behind the doors, in the bath tub, in the fridge, the washing basket, the bread bin, up the trees?"

"Oh, Annie, it's not one bit funny," came the reply. Yes, yes I searched everywhere. What shall we do now? I am so sad."

Great uncle Gerry started to cry. He wanted his little friend back and he did not know how to go about finding him.

"Dear, dear," said Annie as she put her arms around Gerry, to comfort him, "it's going to be all right. Junior did not wander far. He never did before. Don't you start getting yourself upset now, after being so ill. We will find Junior."

What Annie didn't say, is that she had spotted Junior as Gerry drove in. His long black tail was hanging down, under Gerry's car.

"I think I have found him," she said, with even a bigger smile and great excitement.

They all turned to look at the car. Jonnie opened the car bonnet and there sitting inside, as cosy as you like, was Junior, smiling out at him.

When Great Uncle Gerry saw Junior, he was so happy. He lifted him out of the car and cuddled him. Junior purred happily. He was so happy to be in Gerry's arms again.

"My goodness," said Great Uncle Gerry, as he stroked his little friend. "I think we'll have to give you a good wash, when we get home. You smell like diesel, phew, in fact, you smell so much like diesel, I think I am going to name you Diesel." And with that Junior became Diesel. Everyone thought that Diesel was the perfect name. They all laughed. Everyone was glad, that Diesel was safe and sound.

I must tell you that Princess Gwen, Gerry's grandniece, did not think that Diesel was a good name, for a cat but she loved the story. What do you think?

The Nearly-Forgotten Birthday

It was a bright summer morning. The birds were chirping. Sun rays peeped through the bedroom windows of the Royal Palace on Keeper hill.

I think it was on a Saturday in August?

The eight royal grandchildren were at Queen Rainbow's royal palace for a few sleepovers. The children began to wake one by one. First the four girls started to stir. The eldest was, Lola-Rose. She liked to be called Lola. She always woke first and read a little, before the other girls disturbed her. The other three were; Penelope, Gwenevere, who called herself Gwen, and Zoe-Marie, who called herself Zoe. In the next room, they could hear the rumbling and fumbling of the boys. They were so noisy. The eldest was Alexander, who called himself Alex, and the other three were Noah, Isaac and Evan. All eight grandchildren of queen Rainbow and King Jack came to the palace, to spend a couple of days holidays.

The strange and exciting thing about this day, was that it was their birthday. Yes! All of them. They were different ages, but they all had the same birthday. They were all first cousins and they were all royal princes and princesses. Isn't that a wonderful coincidence? Well, it would have been wonderful, had they remembered, but not one of them did. They were having such a nice holiday at the palace, that they had completely forgotten what date it was.

They loved staying at the palace of their grandparents. Queen Rainbow and king Jack had many treats and they were allowed to stay up late and play all day, in the royal gardens.

Now, queen Rainbow knew well, that it was going to be an exciting day and there would be lots of surprises. She could not believe it, when all eight children came into the kitchen and did not mention their birthday. She played along with them.

"Well, good morning," said Queen Rainbow. "Have you thought of something special, you would like to do today."

Some of them said, that they were going into the royal playground, to swing and slide and maybe collect some leaves and flowers for a mud pie.

The others, decided that they were going to play football in, the Royal gardens.

"That sounds wonderful" said queen Rainbow, with a cheeky smile on her face. "Let us have breakfast first."

The children sat down, to a feast of chocolate pancakes, that they had on special occasions and sleepovers. They all loved chocolate pancakes. It was their favourite breakfast.

"Why are we having such a special breakfast?" asked Lola and Penelope.

"Because I love you all so much. You are my very, precious, little grandchildren and it is a speelover."

That was a good reason. They ate all their delicious breakfast. Isaac and Evan, who were the littlest, had chocolate smiles. Noah always seemed to get food on his face, or in his lovely, blond hair. Queen Rainbow thought it was funny, that all eight children didn.t remember, what a wonderful, special day today was. She cleaned their faces. She allowed them, out into the royal gardens and asked them to back at 10.30, for their mid-morning snack. Nani would keep her eyes on them, until then. Thats if Nani didnt fall asleep, which she liked to do, relaxing in the sunshine.

"Be careful out in the royal gardens, she told them. "and please Nani, can you make sure, that the children stay far away from the Royal Fairy Garden. That is out of bounds today, because there are repairs being done. King Jack needs to go to town, to get some supplies. He then has work to do, in the Fairy garden. It will not be safe to play there today."

What the children did not know, was, that while they were playing all morning. King Jack was busy in the Royal fairy garden, preparing a wonderful, birthday celebration, for all eight royal grandchildren. It was going to be a great day.

The children, were happy, after their feast of chocolate pancakes and milk. Three of them, ran to the football garden to play ball. Four hurried off to the royal playground, to swing and slide. Gwen went climbing. She was like a little monkey climbing and swinging up and down, on branches and trees. After what seemed like a long while playing, they were feeling hungry. They heard queen Rainbow ringing the lunch bell.

"Penelope, Lola, Evan, Alex, Zoe, Isaac, Noah and Gwen," Nani called. "You need to come in, out of the hot sun, for a rest and a snack."

The hungry children, raced indoors. They were all laughing and screaming as they ran. After they had washed their hands, they sat around the large, royal table, queen Rainbow appeared, with a big tray of rice-crispy buns. The children gasped with pleasure. These were their favourite buns ever.

"Oh, my goodness! Yummy!" they all said, Alex of course, was the loudest because he loved chocolate, more than anything, even more than Rugby.

"This is a very special treat, grandma Rainbow" said Gwen. "Are you sure, there is nothing special today? I feel, there is something different about today."

"No, not at all, I just love you all so much and you are so kind and caring to each other, every time you are together. I wanted to make you a special treat," Queen Rainbow replied, with a big smile.

She could not reveal, that she had been busy all morning, making a great, big, birthday cake and in the afternoon, she would busy herself wrapping all their presents. King Jack was also very busy, decorating the Fairy Garden with ribbons, lights and balloons and placing nice things to eat, on the party table. It was Nani's job to keep the children busy and far away from the Fairy Garden.

When the children finished their rice-crispy buns, they rested a while. They played a game of I spy with my little eye. Then they went to pick flowers for grandma Rainbow and for their mommies and daddies. Queen Rainbow said, that they could have a late lunch at 3pm on the dot. Then, off the children went, with baskets and buckets, to collect flowers. They mostly collected the heads of flowers and left the stems. They also collected pebbles and leaves. Alex and Lola, who were the oldest, filled buckets with water. Everything ended up, as a big mud pie in the gardener's shiny, new wheelbarrow. Nani stayed with the children, to make sure they were safe. Afterwards, they wandered far down the meadow to the farmers' fields, to watch the cows grazing. It was great fun in the meadow. The freshly, grown grass was soft, like carpet, and long enough to play hide and seek in.

While the children were out, queen Rainbow wrapped their birthday presents. She thought it remarkable, that they all forgot, their very, special day. That was because they were so excited, to be at the Palace and allowed to play together, in the gardens Oh, what a surprise they will get at 3pm, she thought.

She prepared all the presents. For Alex, she wrapped a Minecraft game. For Lola, she had a Tablet. Penelope wanted a rocking horse. Noah was getting the yellow truck, he wished for. For Gwen, the rainbow Teddy, that she asked Nani to knit, was finished just in time. She wrapped a blue car for Isaac, a doll for Zoe, and for little Evan, a baby teddy. The gifts were wrapped in multi-coloured paper with purple, yellow, and red ribbon.

Queen Rainbow then hurried to the Fairy garden, to see how king Jack was getting on, with the birthday party preparations. He was very busy turning the fairy garden into a wonderful birthday garden. He made bows, picked flowers and hung lanterns. Queen Rainbow placed all the presents on the table in the centre of the garden and rushed back, to change into a pretty gown and put on her crown.

The children came back from the meadow, with over flowing baskets, of flowers . They had rose petals, sunflowers, poppies, sweet pea and many more. At fifteen minutes to three, Nani reminded them of the time. They all came rushing into the royal dining hall, expecting a special lunch. They thought queen Rainbow was being extra kind today, for some unknown reason. But there was nothing prepared, no treats to be seen. Not a sausage. Not even a cracker with cheese?

Queen Rainbow entered the dining hall and asked the children to change into clean clothes. She said, that she made a surprise lunch for them, in the Fairy garden. They rushed to their bathrooms. The children washed their hands and faces. Nani helped the boys choose clean clothes and the girls picked their own, because were good at picking. She dressed little Evan, who couldn,t dress himself.

When they were all dressed and clean, they hurried to the Fairy Garden. It was five minutes to three. Tick tock, tick tock. Time was counting down. Alex checked his watch. Four minutes to three. Tick tock, tick tock. They stood at the entrance to the Fairy Garden.

It was very quiet in there. Alex checked his watch again. Three minutes to go. Tick tock, tick tock. Two minutes to go. one minute. It was just seconds now, counting down. Tick tock, tick tock, five, tick tock, four, tick tock, three, tick tock, two, tick tock, tick tock and with that, the gates to the Fairy garden opened. The children ran in and came to a sudden standstill. What a wonderful surprise they got, when they saw the garden. It was beautifully decorated. There were balloons and fairylights. There were sparkles and stars hanging from the trees. It was magical. Their royal parents, baron Michael, baroness Caroline, countess Kasey, earl Mathew, lord Jesse and lady Sara were all there, singing, "Happy birthday".

But where was Nani, they wondered?

There were lots of happy-birthday hugs. King Jack and Queen Rainbow were so pleased, with the preperation of the secret, wonderful day, for the royal children. The children were so happy. They opened their presents and were all very satisfied.

The children still wondered where Nani was, but queen Rainbow told them that she probably got delayed and suggested that, they cut the humongous cake and enjoy the party.

Queen Rainbow, king Jack and all the mommies and daddies sang 'Happy birthday', once again. The children were jumping with joy, as king Jack lit the candles, when all of a sudden there was a big explosion of fireworks and out popped Nani, from the top of the huge cake. There she was on top of the centre of the huge cake, singing.

"Happy birthday to all you wonderful royal children, on this special day. It's the most special day of the year, for you princes and princesses. Penelope, Lola, Evan, Alex, Zoe, Isaac Noah and Gwen, happy birthday to you!"

All the grown-ups sang the birthday song and the children joined in. They ate delicious chocolate cake. They danced around and partied, for a long time.

They stayed in the garden until the sun was beginning to set and the stars were getting ready to twinkle. It was their best birthday ever.

I love to swing so high. What is your favourite thing to play in the garden?

A Fright in the Night

Once upon a hill, there lived three, very special children. Princess Gwen, who sometimes, liked to call herself Goldie-lockets. She was four years old.

Penelope, who liked to be called Snow-white-flakes. She was the biggest and was five and a half.

The littlest was a boy called Isaac, who liked to be called Caleb from time to time. He was just three.

One day,well, in the middle of the night.

I think it was on a Monday in October?

The children, woke to the sound of a loud bang, on the roof, of their bedroom. It was frightening. They never heard a sound like this, before, during the night. They glanced at each other and then looked around the bedroom, to make sure nothing fell off the shelves, or that nothing landed on their cieling window..They checked, to see, if any of their bed buddies were playing around the bedroom.

No, nothing unusual had happened. This was very unusual. Where could that sound have come from? A couple of minutes. later there it was again.

Isaac was the first to check his bed, making sure all his soft toys, were still where he had left them. There was Lamy, Blue Aeroplane, Oxy, Dino, Doggy, Monkey, Duck, Blue Bunny (who was his favourite), Lion and the three cars, that he brought to bed with him, that evening, before mummy tucked him in. He told the girls, that all his toys were in bed, so they were'nt responsible, for the loud bang.

"Mm," Gwen sighed, as she checked that all her bed buddies were in place. There was Brown bunny, Cat, Dog, two dolls called Sweets and Sparkle, Cow, Cow 2, Pink Bunny, Pink Princess Heart, Grey Bunny, Yellow Butterfly and Rag Doll. She smiled at the other two children, feeling so proud that all her bed buddies were behaving themselves, as they usually did and stayed asleep all night. They definitely were not to blame, for the loud noise.

Just then there was another loud crack on the window. The children jumped with fright.

"Maybe, the acorns and horse chestnuts are blowing off the tree in the garden," said Gwen. "It's very windy outside.

"That tree is too far away," said Isaac. "They cannot fall this far and I think I have collected all the conkers."

Something really wasn't right.

"I don't know what that sound could be" said Penelope, who was the eldest, as she checked her bed to see if all her friends, were still in bed. Yes; Grey bunny, Doll, Butterfly cushion, Grey Bunny 2, Grey mousey and Lamb were all clear to be seen. She rumbled through her very, cosy, pink blanket that Nani knit her, to check if the others were hiding and yes, there they were; Cow, Rabbit, Pink Duck, Bunny, Peppa Pig, Sparkly Cushion, Princess Cushion, Monkey and Stripy Elephant. With a sigh of relief, she smiled and told the others, that everyone was there, though were hiding under the pink, cosy blanket because they were scared by the loud noise.

The children decided, that it would not be necessary to wake their parents, since everything and everyone were all in place. Daddy, earl Matthew, and mommy, countess Kasey, slept way down the corridor, out of earshot. None of the three, wanted to walk down, to wake them, so they curled up under their duvets, with all their bed buddies and tried to sleep.

There was silence. Then there was another loud bang. Then a loud cry. Penelope screamed!

"Pink Mousey, Pink Mousey, where is my Pink Mousey, oh where, oh where could she be?" Penelope cried, as she rumbled through her bed buddies. Her pink blanket was shaken. Under the bed was thoroughly searched. She ran frantically around the bedroom, searching and crying.

"She is gone, Oh no, Where could she be?" cried Penelope, as tears rolled down her cheeks. Pink Mousey had been with Penelope, since the day she was born. She was a little shabby, from all the washing. She was patched and stitched many times but that didn't matter. Penelope loved her so much.

She searched and she searched. Gwen and Isaac were wide awake now. They searched under their blankets and under their beds, but they could not find Pink Mousey.

"Oh, dearie me" said Gwen. "She is really not here in our beds, let's try the drawers and the window sills. Let's try everywhere."

The children searched. They pulled all their underwear, tops and socks out of the drawers and scattered them, all over the bedroom floor. They pulled all their dress-up outfits from the pink basket and threw them in a pile, in the middle of the bedroom floor. They took their clothes, from the hangers and threw them, in the middle. Lastly, they emptied the big tub, where they kept their toy golf set, their hobby horses, princess wands and their long bubble-maker-sticks. They chucked them into the big heap, in the middle of the bedroom floor. Penelope cried even louder.

"She is gone, oh no, where could she be," cried Penelope, as the tears rolled down her cheeks.

She searched and she searched. The other two searched also, under their blankets and under their beds, but they could not find Pink Mousey.

"Oh, dearie me" said Gwen, "She is really not here in our beds. Let us try everywhere, again."

The children, searched again, through the heap, on the bedroom floor.

"Oh, my goodness" said the voice, at the bedroom door. Mommy was standing there. Before they could explain, Mommy said, in not-such-a-pleasant voice.

"What on earth are you three villains doing, in these small hours of the morning, playing with all your toys and throwing your clothes, around your bedroom. It's going to take all night to tidy them,. we won't have had enough sleep and we wanted to go to the beach tomorrow. Mmm I think we will have to stay home and tidy, all day."

"Well I don't want to go to the beach," cried Penelope. "Not without my Pink Mousey and I cannot, I mean, we cannot find her anywhere. There was a loud noise and we all woke up. We checked, to see if all our bed buddies were ok. We went back to sleep and then I remembered, my most precious buddy of all, who I have had since I was a baby. She was not in my bed, like she always is and she is always with me, so now I don't ever want to go to the beach, or do anything again, without her and I don't care and, and, and," she broke down in floods of tears.

"Oh, dear me," said mommy. "that is just the worst news ever." We must find Pink Mousey at once," she said, as she gave Penelope a big hug.

Just then, Daddy appeared at the door, in wonderment, at mommy hugging Penelope, in the middle of the bedroom, in a muddle of toys, clothes and everyone being upset.

"What on earth happened here, was there an earthquake, I didn't hear an earthquake. Or maybe a train drove through this bedroom?" said Daddy jokingly. "Penelope, you woke me up with all your sobbing. What on earth is going on and why is this room such a mess?"

"Oh Daddy," said Gwen, in one long breath. "Pink Mousey is gone missing and there was a loud bang and we all woke up and we searched everywhere, for all our bed buddies. We found all of them, except, Pink Mousey. She is the only one, we cannot find and then there was another loud bang and then Mommy came in and now you came in and we still can't find her."

"Calm down, children," said Daddy in a quiet gentle voice. "Are you sure you brought Pink Mousey to bed, Penelope?"

"Yes, of course I did. She is always with me and she always sleeps with me."

"Well are you sure you tucked her in, after brushing your teeth and after your good-night stories? Think really hard now and try to remember."

Then, came another loud bang. It was not as loud as the first, but loud enough to startle everyone and make them jump.

"Goodness me," said Daddy. "What on earth was that strange, loud noise? It sounded like it came from the roof. But there cannot be anyone on the roof. It is slanted and they would roll off."

Just then there was another loud noise at the roof window.

"Are you sure you tucked Pink Mousey in?" asked Daddy again.

Well, Penelope thought, we were out looking at the night sky, before bedtime. Gwen had Brown bunny, Isaac had Blue Bunny and I had Pink Mousey. "Remember Daddy," said Penelope. "We watched the north star and the full moon and all twinkling stars. You held the big torch, so that we could see where we were walking."

"That's true," Daddy said. "But you,carried the torch, Penelope, remember and you laid Pink Mousey, on the bench. Maybe she is still lying there, in the cold?"

Penelope could not bear the thought of her precious Pink Mousey, lying outside in the cold dark night, even though it was very nice, to be out under the stars and the full moon. It was a disaster.

Just then, there was another noise at the window. Daddy stood on Gwen's bed. It was the nearest bed, to the window and he could reach up to open and stick his head out. He looked around by the light of the full moon. He could clearly see all around the roof. There was no one to be seen. Just then he heard a little voice.

"I'm down here. I am finding it difficult, to find big stones to attract attention. I'm trying to wake someone, to come and fetch me."

Penelope heard the voice of her favourite cuddle toy and she sobbed. She was so sad.

"I hear you Pink Mousey, I hear you. I am so sorry, that I left you out in the cold and dark. I am so sorry, that I forgot to tuck you in. but I was so tired after our adventurous day, that I slept very quickly and did not miss you. I am so sorry Pink Mousey. I will take really good care of you, from now on. I will never go to sleep without you again."

As Penelope was still talking out the window to her friend, daddy rushed down to the garden, to fetch Pink Mousey. Penelope was so happy when he appeared again, in the room, with a very cold and shivering Pink Mousey.

The whole family jumped for joy. Mommy hugged Gwen. Daddy hugged Isaac. Penelope gave her cuddly friend, the biggest cuddle ever. She promised, that she would never again, forget to bring Pink Mousey in from the garden.

Mommy and Daddy tucked the three children into bed, wished them a good night and went back to their own bedroom. The children curled up, under their warm duvets. Isaac held Blue Bunny close, Gwen held Brown Bunny even closer and Penelope held Pink Mousey, like she would never let her go. The big heap of toys and clothes, was left in the middle of the bedroom floor. They were all, too exhausted to tidy away. It would have to wait until morning. Everyone was glad, that no harm came, to Pink Mousey and she was reunited with her best friend, Penelope. They cuddled very tight that night and every night after. Next morning, they woke bright and early and tidied away the mess on their bedroom floor. They all had a great day at the beach.

Do you have a favourite toy or a favourite bed buddie?

One Day the Children Went to Pick Flowers

It was one bright sunny day on Keeper hill and it was Mommy's birthday. The children wanted to surprise her, with a vase of freshly, picked flowers.

I think it was on a Monday in July?

The three children living in Sleeper cottage Castle went to pick flowers. Penelope was just four years old. Her little sister Gwen, was three and their brother Isaac, was two. They wanted to pick Mommy pretty flowers. They loved to stroll down the lane and run through the tree tunnels.

Off they went, the two sisters with their little baskets. Isaac did not have a basket. He always put his flowers in the girls baskets. He wanted his hands free, so the he could get up to mischief and see Barney, the bull, at the end of the lane. Barney ate nuts and straw at lunchtime, every day. The girls had to hold Isaac's hands, most of the time. Barney, the bull, looked funny chewing, with his big tongue wobbling in and out, of his huge mouth. Isaac and the girls loved to watch him, gobbling all his food.

The girls liked to watch butterflies land on the many, colourful flowers along the lane. There were tiny pink roses, yellow gorse, red lanterns and blue bells. Gwen loved yellow flowers, because, yellow was her favourite colour. Penelope preferred pink or red flowers. They let go of Isaac's hands, while placing the flowers in their baskets and forgot, to hold his hands again. I think Nani would have something to say about that. She always warned the girls, to keep hold of his hands, even if he didn't want them to.

They wandered down the lane, collecting a great selection of petals, filling their baskets almost to the top and listening to the sweet, sounds of the birds on their way. The flowers and petals were so light, that their baskets never got too heavy to carry, even though they were almost full. They liked to climb on the farmer's gate and gaze out, over the vastness of Keeper valley below. They could see green fields and blue hills, in the distance. They saw the school down in Rainbow village. There were children playing in the school football field. The girls looked forward to the day, when they could attend big school.

They walked, for a short while, collecting pretty flowers, when they realised, that Isaac was not behind them, or in front of them for that matter. He may have run on ahead to see Barney bull, but they couldn't see him.

"Oh, my goodness, said Penelope. where has our little brother wandered off to? He is always up to mischief, always running off and hiding."

They called out his name, a few times.

"Isaac, Isaac, where are you?" they called out as loud as they could, even though Nani always told them, that little girls should be seen, and not heard. But this was an exception to the rule, so they shouted louder, but there was no reply.

The girls, walked a little further, down the lane but they could not see him. They thought of turning back, but changed their minds and kept going, towards Barney bull, constantly calling Isaac's name very loudly.

"Where could he be gone off to now?" asked Gwen, as she spotted robin redbreast, high up on a big branch, singing his heart out.

"Hey Robin, our little brother has run off. Have you seen him?"

"Tweet, tweet," replied the robin. "He is always running off and always up to mischief. He is very good at hiding, but I have not seen him and don't know where he is, sorry."

"My goodness," said Penelope, as she called his name and wondered where he could have gone.

"Mr Cow," she called, as she passed where the cows were grazing, "Have you seen Isaac? He is gone missing again. Every time we come out to pick flowers, he runs off. Can you please help us?"

"Moo!" said Mr. cow. "He passed this way a little while ago with a very mischievous look on his face. He would not tell me, where he was going, but he looked like he was going that way."

Mr. cow pointed towards the tree tunnel.

"Or maybe it was that way, as he pointed towards home."

"Well, that wasn't much help," said Gwen. "We will just have to use our own common sense and presume that he is gone to see Barney bull"

The girls were a little worried, that Isaac, would wander into the fields and not find his way home. He was still very little. They called his name over and over. But he did not answer.

Farmer Mike passed in his big, yellow tractor as, they walked under a tree tunnel. He waved to the girls and then stopped, when he realised, that Isaac was not with them.

"Where have you left your brother?" asked farmer Mike, in his very deep voice. "Is he sleeping?"

"I wish he was," Gwen. "Then we would not have to worry about him. He ran off again and we cannot find him. I suppose, we shouldn't have let go of his hand."

"Oh, he is probably gone home, hiding somewhere in the garden," said farmer Mike. "Don't worry too much. He never wanders far away. I have just been with Barney bull. He is not there."

"Well, you have been a great help, farmer Mike. Thank you so much," smiled Gwen.

The girls waved goodbye to Farmer Mike and walked home, calling Isaac all the way. They passed the deer in the meadow and asked if they had spotted their brother, but no luck there. They had not seen him either.

The girls stopped for a while. They climbed up on the big, green gate that kept the cows in their field. They saw the whole of Keeper Valley from there, Rainbow village and Miss Weed, pottering away at her flowers. They saw far away fields and the very, tip, top of great uncle Gerry's blue mansion in the distance.

"It is truly wonderful to live here," said Gwen. They both gazed for a while and took in the fresh country air. Sometimes, country air was very smelly. They called that 'farmer-perfume'.

"Yes, it is truly wonderful," Penelope agreed.

After a short while, the girls strolled, towards home. When they arrived at the wooden gates to their garden, they called out to Isaac again. Then they heard a quiet voice from way up at the top of the garden.

"Hi girls, I'm up here. I tricked you!" said Isaac and laughed very loudly. "I ran back home and came up here to the garden. Come on you two."

"Where on earth is he now, maybe he is up in a tree," said Gwen.

"Up here on the swing. Here I am!" he shouted and laughed again, heartily, as he swung, very high indeed.

"Oh, you are a silly boy," Penelope said, as she and Gwen ran up the hill behind the house to the playground.

All three sat on the swings. They looked, over the trees and down into the valley. They saw the castles, where their cousins lived. They saw the deep, blue sea. It was such a magnificent view.

The children, played on the swings for a while. They then jumped on the trampoline, tumbling backwards and forwards. They had so much fun, laughing and playing together, that Isaac's mischief, was quickly forgotten. After play time, they brought Mommy her flowers. She was very happy and they all looked forward to a delicious slice of her birthday cake.

What colour flowers are your favorite?

Oxy and Jammy

It started one day, just before spring in the land of Truth and happiness. Well, actually, between the land of Truth and Happiness and Blue Island. Jammy, the bigbrown bear, sat on his rock, like he did every day and looked towards the ocean, wondering what it would be like, to live under the sea.

I think it was on a Thursday in February?

Oxy, the pink and purple octopus, sat on a strand of seaweed and looked rowards the shore. Oxi, liked living in the ocean, with all her fish friends. There was Shelly Shark, Lily Lobster, Dandy Dolphin, Curly Crab and lots more. She loved to spend time under water, swimming around, but one thing she really wished she could do, at least once in her life, was to take a trip on land. Every day she sat on her patch of seaweed, with waves crashing over her. She looked longingly, towards the shore. She wanted to go there one day, to smell flowers, see the trees and meet the animals of the land and to meet the royal children of Keeper Queendom. They often came to the beach, to play and swim and picnic.

Today was a cold sunny day. Oxy had a clear view towards the shore. She was a little sad. Then, she saw, someone or something sitting on a big rock on the beach. She swam forward to investigate. There, sitting under the shade of a palm tree, was a big brown furry animal. He looked sad and forlorn.

Jammy was a big jolly brown bear. He loved honey and the sea. He also liked, stomping around the forest, smelling flowers and splashing in the river, but most of all, he loved his friends and honey. There was Rodger robin, Sammy squirrel, Harry horse and many more. The one thing Jammy wished he could do, was someday, swim in the big ocean, under the deep blue sea. He sat every morning on his rock, near the shore, well only when there were no people about. He listened to the waves rolling in and out, in and out. Jammy loved to watch fish jump and boats sailing on the horizon. He could see as far as Blue Island, where the sharks and penguins lived. On this particular morning, Jammy was sadder than usually. It was, because the sun was shining on the water and the waves looked so wonderful. He really wanted to know what went on, under the deep blue sea.

Then, to his surprise, he saw someone swimming towards the shore. It was a pink and purple octopus. Jammy waved to her a few times, from where he sat. He ran towards the water's edge. He was so excited at the possibility of meeting someone, from the deep blue sea. He shouted out.

"Hi there," I am Jammy, brown bear from the Land of Truth and Happiness."

"Hi Jammy. My name is Oxy. You don't look too happy today. Can I help cheer you up?" enquired Oxy. "We could sing songs to each other, or tell jokes. I live under the sea, with all my friends. I would like to go out of the water to your land, but even though I have eight arms, I have no legs, to walk on. I have to stay here in the water."

"Oh, that's a shame," shouted Jammy. "I would love to go into the water. I could be your best friend, but I am very big and awkward and I never learned how to swim. I have to stay here on dry land."

They chatted for a little while, about their different lives. Jammy spoke about, birds and other animals. Oxy told Jammy, about the different types of fish. They loved each other's company. Before saying goodbye, they both gazed longingly at each other, for a while.

That night, Oxy slept very deep. She dreamt that she swam, above the water and over the green Land of Truth and Happiness and through the trees, along the river and over the mountains. Next morning, she was so excited. She couldn't wait to tell Jammy. She shouted from her seaweed, the minute she saw him on the shore.

"Hey Jammy, I dreamt that I was swimming, over the water, in the air. It was wonderful. Oh, how I wish I could."

Jammy thought hard for a little while.

"Well, maybe, you can. If you swim a little closer to the shore and reach out to me, with your eight arms, I will catch you and carry you, on my strong back. I can show you where I live. Let's try it. I'm coming closer to you. I can carry you on my strong back and take you, to the Land of Truth and Happiness."

Oxy swam, with great caution in the shallow water, as far inland as she could. Jammy paddled into the water, splashing with every step until he was very close to Oxy. He helped her wiggle, on to his back. She held on very tightly, with her eight arms and he splashed back to shore. Jammy took Oxy, on the most exciting adventure. He ran through the forest and showed her the green trees, shrubs and daffodils. He introduced her to all his friends. She said hello to, Sammy squirrel, Harry horse, Rodger hobin and Farmer mike. He took her all over Keeper hill and down into the valley. He called by the palace, to see the royal children and introduced her, to all eight of them. He sat on the swing. He went down to the meadow to greet the cows. He let her taste some of his bread and honey, his favourite food. They met reindeer, sheep, dogs and rabbits. He ran through Rainbow village. He called out, hello, to all the nice people. He travelled with Oxy on his back, for hours and hours. Night was falling. Jammy was sleepy.

"I have to return you, to the deep blue sea," he said. "It's time for me to go to bed. I'm so tired after such a long day."

Jammy, brought Oxy back to the shore, dropped her gently, into the cool water and waved goodbye.

Oxy thanked Jammy over and over. She was so happy. He made her dream came true and it was all she imagined it would be. She was so happy to return to the deep blue sea. She needed to swim a little, to stretch and loosen her body and her eight legs, that were stiff, from sitting on Jammy's back all day. She swam deep, under the water and told her friends, about her great adventure. She slept very well that night. She dreamt of her wonderful adventure and her new friend.

Next morning, Oxy swam to the shore to meet her new friend. Jammy was nowhere to be seen. She called his name but he did not come. She sat a while on her seaweed, feeling a little sad. She hoped that nothing had happened to Jammy, her new best friend.

After an hour, Jammy came running, out of breath and waving and calling her. He looked very anxious.

"What is the matter, Jammy," she called out.

"I was so tired after carrying you all day yesterday, I slept for a very long time," he explained. "I thought I would miss you Oxy. I have to tell you, that I had a dream last night. In my dream, I could swim in the deep blue sea. It was so amazing. I was in the water, even though I cannot really swim."

"Then come on Jammy, why don't you come closer to the water? Catch one or two of my arms! I will take you to the deep blue sea."

Jammy was so excited, he forgot about being scared of the water. He ran so fast towards the water, that he tripped over in the sand and landed on his head. Bump, it didn't bother him. He splashed with his big feet, into the shallow water, frightening many little fish. When he got close to Oxy, he reached out and caught hold of her arms.

"Are you secure, she asked. Are you ready to swim?"

"Yes," Jammy replied. He was scared and excited. He had butterflies, in his tummy. Oxy, took off like a rocket, down under the water. Jammy could barely hold on.

"Not so fast," he called out and they both laughed. Oxy swam through the coral and sea grass, through the underwater caves and the schools of tiny fish. They met her friends and said hello, to Willy whale, Larry and Carrie crab, who thought it was so funny to see a big, hairy, animal swimming down under the water. They swam to Blue Island and greeted the grumpy, sharks and the laughing penguins. They sat on a rock, for a chat, with the pink flamingos.

Oxy invited Jammy for tea, but Jammy said, "Uh, I don't think a few shrimps will fill me. I will have to go home and get yummy honey."

"Oh, but we have fresh salmon here also," said Oxy.

"Well, in that case, I will stay for tea," said Jammy, rubbing his tummy.

He filled his belly with tasty, juicy salmon, before Oxy brought him back to shore. It was more difficult for Oxy carrying Jammy back, after his big feast, of salmon. He was a lot heavier, but she was a great swimmer and the water, took some of his weight.

They said goodbye and promised each other to do that again, very soon. It was the best day Jammy ever had, in his whole life. He was looking forward to the next time he could travel with Oxy. He slept very soundly that night and dreamt about his great adventure, under the sea.

Next morning the two friends met again, Jammy on the shore under the palm tree and Oxy on her seaweed, near the water's edge. They waved to each other and smiled lovingly. Both friends knew, that they would go on more adventures together, whenever they wished. They were truly happy. Both their dreams had come true, with help from each other. That's what good friends are for, to help each other, when they can.

Do you have a best friend?

Nani's Little Red Car

Part 1

It started one day after it had snowed and sleeted on the Queendom of Keeper Hill. All the royal parents and grandparents had to go out, for the day. Nani arrived at Sleeper cottage, to take care of the royal children.

I think it was on a Wednesday in December?

Prince Isaac, just two years old, climbed up on the giant, purple bean bag, that was propped up against the window. He looked out and saw, that Nani's little red car, was parked in the drive. The car looked more sparkly than usual. It was so red, against the white snow, which was melting very quickly, forming muddy puddles in the driveway. Nani said, she had been to the car wash and had her red car cleaned and polished. It sparkled like new.

Nani always parked her car in the drive. She put the keys in her pocket, but she never locked the car doors.

Isaac's, two sisters, princess Penelope and princess Gwen, who were just four, and three years old, were in the play room, drawing with their new, magic markers.

Isaac called his two sisters. "Penelope, Gwen, come and see Nani's sparkling car."

They both stopped colouring and joined Isaac, on the purple, maxi Buddabag The children gasped in amazement, when they saw how pretty Nani's car looked. It was different, not just red like every other day. No, today it sparkled and twinkled like treasure. The lights were shining and it had a smile, on its bonnet face. It winked to the children. Oh! They looked at each other in wonderment, then looked back again to the red car. It winked again. The children got a shiver of excitement.

The rain and sleet, which had been pouring down all morning, had finally stopped. They asked Nani, if they could go out to play. They had been playing inside all morning, because of the bad weather. Nani helped them, put on their raincoats and wellies. Penelope put on her red princess wellies, Gwen put on yellow princess wellies and Isaac had blue Spiderman wellies. Nani allowed them, to go out and play in the drive, so that she could see them from the kitchen window. She gave them buckets and coloured boxes and wooden shovels. She went back in the house to prepare lunch. She knew they would be safe there, because the big gates, which led to the country road, where farmer Mike drives his tractor, were closed. The gates could only be opened, by remote control, or with a big key. The children kept busy, with stones and buckets and things, they found. Nani watched them, from the kitchen. She checked from time to time, that they were playing and not in any danger. She asked them, to stay, where she could see them.

Isaac climbed into the red car. He sat on the driver's seat and pretended to drive. He was enjoying this, until he heard a wierd sound, like humming or whistling. He looked in the back seat, the passenger seat and the glove compartment. He couldn't see anything or anyone, who could have made such a sound. He listened again. He heard a curious sound, just like before. Then he heard a whispering voice.

"Drive me Isaac,"said a voice, from the steering wheel.

Isaac could not believe his ears. He called his sisters.

"Hey girls, come here. You won't believe it. Nani's red car is magic. She can sing and speak."

The girls shrugged their shoulders in disbelief, as they climbed into the red car. They both looked at Isaac curiously.

"Well then, Isaac?" they asked.

"Speak again," commanded Isaac, but there was not a sound.

"Well Isaac?" said the girls again, mockingly.

"Please speak little, red car?" cried Isaac.

There was no sound for a little while. Then, they heard.

"I am a magic car. If you like, you can take me for a drive. In fact, anything you want to do, you just need to ask."

Isaac smiled his brightest and biggest smile, to his sisters, delighted that they knew, he was not imagining it. The girls nodded their heads in approval.

"Are you sure?" asked Isaac. "anything?"

"Yes, I am," was the reply from the little red car.

"Ok," said Isaac. Let's go on an adventure."

Gwen said yes, right away. Penelope wasn't absolutely sure about this at first, but she then agreed.

The gates were closed. They wondered, how they could open them.

"Little red car," Isaac said, with such excitement."Open the gates."

The heavy wooden gates opened.

"Drive little red car," commanded Isaac.

The car huffed and puffed and started its engine. It drove slowly and carefully out the gates, turned left and drove down the long, country road, under the tree tunnels and past some deer.

The children jumped with joy, as the little red car bumped in and out of the muddy puddles. They shouted to the deer in the field, that they were going on an adventure. They waved to the robins on the trees. They passed three, mammy cows and their baby calves.

"Moo,"said the cows.

"Moo" shouted the children in return, as they bumped along.

Birds sang. Deer ran in the meadow, when they spotted the little red car. The sun rays were pouring through the clouds. There were patches of blue sky to be seen. There would be no more snow or rain today. The children were having so much fun. Then, the car came to a sudden stop. It was stuck, in the biggest, muddiest puddle ever. The puddle was twice as big as the car. The children screamed with excitement, when they saw it. They were glad, they had their wellies on. They stepped carefully out of the car, into the big puddle. They splashed and danced and jumped with both feet, as hard and as high as they could, especially Isaac, who always danced with both feet, in every muddy puddle he could find. He always got his trousers and socks wet. They danced and splashed and sang, for quite a while, until they heard Nani's voice calling their names. Oh no, they were in trouble.

"Penelope, Gwen, Isaac, where are you?"

Oh! She did not look happy, as she came thundering towards them. They were just about to tell her about their adventure, when suddenly, the little, red car disappeared, just like that, into thin air and the muddy puddle they were jumping about in, decreased in size. The children gasped with disbelief. They could not tell Nani about what had happened. How could they explain, with the red car missing and the muddy puddle now, so small? They could not explain, how the gates opened either.

"Just look at you, all wet and happy. How on earth did you walk all this way, by yourselves and so fast? My goodness, I'm in serious trouble for letting you out. I don't know what, your parents will say, when they get home. I wonder who left those gates open. How careless of those grown-ups."

"Someone must have opened them by mistake," said Penelope. She was four years old since just last week and she was very clever and quick-thinking. She thought of this excuse right away.

"I'll have to speak with queen Rainbow and king Jack. They were the last to leave. They forgot to close those gates securely, or maybe it was mom Kasey and dad Matthew? I'll have to clarify this later," said Nani.

"How careless of someone, to leave the gates open," she repeated.

"Oh, I don't think it was Mom or Dad or any of the royals," said Penelope frantically, very aware, that her parents never leave the gates open by mistake.

"It must have been the postman," she offered in explanation.

"Mm, maybe the postman," Nani said, as she shook her head in disbelief.

She beckoned the three children, to follow her, in the direction of home.

The children glanced at each other in confusion, but didn't utter a single word. They followed Nani along the road, splashing in little, muddy, puddles but we all know what they were thinking.

Where had Nani's red car vanished to?

Part 2

In Keeper Queendom, there was a picturesque village, down in the valley, called Rainbow village. It got its name from queen Rainbow, who ruled the entire queendom. This was where the royals did their shopping. The village supermarket was run by Little, Miss Mix, who was a tiny little lady. She wore a red coat and a purple spotty hat, when she was out walking. She had curly, red hair and always wore pretty clothes. She was very kind. She had a happy face. She was very busy on this day, packing all the shelves with cereal, eggs, crackers and washing powder, when all of a sudden, she heard a strange noise. She thought it was the wind whirling outside. Suddenly, the doors of her supermarket flew open and in drove Nani's red car.

"Well I never," cried Little Miss Mix. "I never saw the like of this in my life. What on earth is a red car doing, in my supermarket?"

The red car huffed and puffed a little, then smiled at Little, Miss Mix and came to a standstill. The engine was very quiet.

"I need some crackers and cheese," said the little red car.

"But you can't eat crackers," replied Little, Miss Mix.

"They are not for me. It is lunchtime and there are no crackers in the house. The boy loves crackers. I need some raisins and apples, for the blond girl and some sausages and strawberries for the dark, haired girl. Oh! and some ice cream, please." "Well I never," repeated Little Miss Mix, once again. "I never heard of a car doing shopping," she said. Then she asked, "who on earth were the boy and the girls. Do they not have names?"

"Oh, I'm sorry, I meant to say prince Isaac, princess Gwen and princess Penelope, the royal grandchildren of course and I am Nani's red car."

"But where is Nani and where are the children?" enquired Little, Miss Mix, with concern. "It is very strange to see you here, without them."

"I know," said the little red car. "I was taking the children, on an adventure. They were in the humongous, muddy, puddle. Nani came looking for them, for lunch but they need some groceries, for lunch. Nani will wonder, how the children got out and they probably can't tell her, that I opened the gates. She will be totally confused."

"Well," replied Little, Miss Mix. "Not half as confused, as I am at this moment. That's a silly story, if ever I heard one."

"It is strange for a car to do the shopping," she remarked as she packed all the groceries, into the back seat.

"It really is a long story, Little, Miss Mix. I'll have to tell you the rest, another time. I must hurry back, before the children miss me. They are splashing in the big, muddy, puddle and Nani is on her way."

Little, Miss Mix looked very confused. She was so confused, that she forgot to say, what a marvellous day it was, like she usually did. "In the big muddy puddle," she said. "And Nani on her way, where?"

"I can't explain now, I have to go!" The little, red car started his engine and left the super market. Little, Miss Mix didn't know what to think. Such a strange happening, she thought, as she waved goodbye to the little, red car. She was all confused. She was in a right muddle and could not remember what she had been doing, before her peculiar visitor arrived. She thought of calling Doctor Brian but she decided instead, to make a nice, cup of tea for herself and relax for a while, until she was over the shock.

The little red car drove out the doors of the supermarket, down the main street of Rainbow village, stopping only once, when the lights were red and going even faster, when the lights turned green again. He drove out of the village, onto the busy road and into the country road. He had to stop once behind Farmer Mike and his big, yellow tractor. As soon as the tractor turned into a field of cows, the little red car, took off again. He drove very quickly along the road, under the bridge of the motorway, passed the big, thatched, cottage at the corner and up Keeper hill. He turned into the country road, bumped over the muddy puddles, said 'beep beep' to the cows and greeted the birds.

He stopped suddenly when he saw, that his big, muddy puddle had vanished and the children too. He drove on and saw, that the wooden gates on the drive, were closed. He commanded the gates to open, drove in and parked. He was very confused, just like Little Miss Mix. He stayed silent for a while and then, in a soft voice, started to beep. Nothing happened. He started to sing softly and beep again. The children were indoors playing. How was he going to get their attention?

Part 3

Nani was in the kitchen, wondering what to prepare for lunch. The children were busy in the playroom. They heard the soft 'beep, beep' and singing. They climbed onto the maxi purple *Buddabag* and looked out the window. To their surprise, Nani's little red car was back in the drive, winking at them. The little red car opened it's back door, to show the children what he had bought at the supermarket.

"Nani is never going to let us out," they said to the little red car. "She will not believe us, if we tell her that you went to the supermarket, to do shopping. What are we going to do?"

"Princess Penelope, being the oldest, had a very clever plan.

"Gwen," she whispered to her younger sister,"you distract Nani and keep her talking in the kitchen. Tell her you are thirsty and you need a drink ortwo drinks, or three drinks. Isaac, keep watch near the door and hold it open, in case Nani comes out of the kitchen. I will run out and fetch the groceries."

Penelope opened the door and sneaked quickly out to the drive, while Isaac kept watch. Penelope took the things from the back seat. She thanked the little red car. She returned to the kitchen, just as Nani was saying that there were no crackers or cheese for lunch and asking Gwen, if she is going to drink the tap dry..

"Oh," said Penelope. "I have some cracker and cheese here. I also have apples, sausages, raisins and ice cream."

"And where did you get them young lady?"

"Oh, Mom must have left them, in the back seat of your, red car" she said.

Nani shook her head in again, in total confusion.

"I don't understand. In the back of my car, Why would she do such a thing? It is all very strange, indeed. I have a lot of questions for your Mom and Dad, when they come home, this evening. They need to hear about the strange things, that have been happening here today. I hope they can explain the gate being left open and how the groceries got into, the back seat of my car."

She shook her head and pursed her lips. "I suppose we should all sit down and enjoy lunch. I'm very confused now. I can think about all those things, after I have had a nice cup of tea."

The children enjoyed their cheese and crackers and all the other things, that the little, red, car had brought them. They didn't dare ask, if they could have ice cream after lunch. They didn't mind though. They giggled quietly, knowing that Nani's red car, was magic and she didn't even know it herself. This would be their greatest secret ever. They smiled fondly at each other, across the table. They looked forward, to many more adventures with Nani's little, red, car.

What do you think Mommy and daddy will say when the come home?

Printed in the United States
By Bookmasters